30 Years
of *Publishing*

HUMAN

HUMAN

Aude

Translated by
Nora Alleyn

Exile Editions

30 YEARS OF PUBLISHING

1976 - 2006

Library and Archives Canada Cataloguing in Publication

Aude, date
[Quelqu'un. English]
 Human / Aude ; translated by Nora Alleyn.

Translation of: Quelqu'un.

ISBN 1-55096-007-5

 I. Alleyn, Nora II. Title. III. Title: Quelqu'un. English.

PS8589.I77Q4413 2006   C843'.54   C2006-906039-8

Original french edition published by XYZ éditeur

Design and Composition by Homunculus ReproSet
Typeset in Galliard, Cochin and Hoefler at the Moons of Jupiter Studios
Printed in Canada by Gauvin Imprimerie

The publisher would like to acknowledge the financial assistance of
The Canada Council for the Arts and the Ontario Arts Council.

Conseil des Arts
du Canada
Canada Council
for the Arts

ONTARIO ARTS COUNCIL
CONSEIL DES ARTS DE L'ONTARIO

This edition published in Canada in 2006 by Exile Editions Ltd.
144483 Southgate Road 14
General Delivery
Holstein, Ontario, N0G 2A0
info@exileeditions.com
www.ExileEditions.com

Canadian Sales Distribution:
McArthur & Company
c/o Harper Collins
1995 Markham Road
Toronto, ON M1B 5M8
toll free: 1 800 387 0117

U.S. Sales Distribution:
Independent Publishers Group
814 North Franklin Street
Chicago, IL 60610
www.ipgbook.com
toll free: 1 800 888 4741

To all those whom I love.

To Denise, my sister,
and to Jean-Guy, my brother,
who left too soon.

To Danielle,
buried alive inside her body.

*Every man carries within himself the
entire form of the human condition.*

— MONTAIGNE

Part One

I started to believe that
only the body counts.
I search for the philosophic stone
in the secret folds of the body.
The exact site of the soul
is the object of my quest.

— RICHARD SELZER

Her name is Jeanne.

The name tag is compulsory. It is pinned to her green hospital gown. Dr. Jeanne Deblois. As if she could forget her own name or not remember it if someone asked her.

Every time she comes into the solarium, it is supposedly to take a break from the busy life of the hospital. In reality, though, she comes to see the woman they wheel in every morning, and wheel back to her room around seven every evening.

Jeanne Deblois doesn't even work in this unit. At first, she came only occasionally, on her way from the operating room or after her rounds on the fifth floor. Now, she comes almost every morning, sometimes several times a day.

Few people venture into the west wing on the top floor of the hospital. Unless they have to. Not only does everyone prefer to avoid this department – most of them act as if it doesn't even exist.

Those who work here are marked by a taboo. As if they had crossed some hidden line, and have come to represent the powerlessness of medicine, of science in general and of the nursing staff in particular. The concrete manifestation of defeat. Of failure.

Everywhere else in the hospital an all-out war is being waged to save lives. The weapons are scalpels, infusions, blood transfusions, smart medications, antibiotics, powerful chemotherapy programs, ablations, amputations, transplants, heart stations, resuscitators. All these procedures are backed up with highly sophisticated technology equipped to track down Evil, flush it out of hiding, irradiate and eradicate it.

Except here in the west wing of the sixth floor. Here, there is no intervention. Here Evil is allowed to invade, to wreak havoc until nothing is left. Here the unwritten rule dictates that patients must consent to this devastation, this annihilation.

Jeanne comes here because of the woman. Immobile, silent, incapable of speech, she is sequestered in this unit as if inside a tomb, inside a body which has become a sarcophagus.

When the day begins, someone wheels her into the room and parks her there, often with her back to the view she might enjoy of the river or the tree tops. Her presence must in no way obstruct hospital traffic. It's not only the chair that upsets the routine. The sight of this woman, her silence, are also deeply disturbing.

One day, Jeanne decided to move the woman's chair over to the window so she could see the bridge and the river swirling beneath it. She didn't dare look at the woman's face. Or speak to her. She came up from behind, pushed the chair, then took a seat some distance away.

She has been repeating this procedure every day for three weeks, always the same way, sometimes giving her a view of the woods, the bicycle path, the busy city; sometimes the river or the park.

She is about to do it again. This morning, after finishing her coffee and watching the sun at play in the autumn leaves, she decided to give the motionless woman a view of the trees so she can follow the sun's flaming trajectory through the bright yellow leaves, throughout the endless succession of hours.

Standing up, Jeanne silently approaches the big blue chair. Her hands are about to reach for the handles when a muffled growl escapes from the woman, the same kind of noise she makes when she chokes, but fiercer, denser. It sounds just like some restless beast.

Jeanne freezes. Could this woman, whom she is only trying to please, be manifesting her irritation in the only way she knows?

Disconcerted, Jeanne heads for the door.

Another growl, short, massive, brutal, forced out with great effort and determination.

Jeanne stops in her tracks. She never expected this reaction, this connection, this summons. She thought she was the only one here who was free to act. She is the one in control of the contact, convinced that her action is correct and necessary under the circumstances, sure of her own benevolent intention.

Up until now, Jeanne has been spying on this patient, shamelessly, whenever she pleases, always placing herself where the other woman can't see her or return her gaze. Jeanne would move the blue chair without ever consulting its occupant. No warning, not so much as a gesture, smile, or word, much less a look that might have engaged the woman's attention in some way.

Unable to go on acting as if nothing has happened, Jeanne could slip away, unnoticed. After all, there's no one here who can prevent her.

Instead, however, she slowly retraces her steps. And now, for the first time, she stands facing the woman.

The eyes are so charged with vehemence that Jeanne has to look away, and for a few seconds she feels distraught, confused.

When visual contact resumes, the woman, with a simple movement of the eyes, directs her to sit down in the chair opposite.

Jeanne sits. And remains seated. Silent. And allows herself to be looked at.

She brushes away the tears that have started to well up, despite herself. She sniffles. Gropes for a handkerchief she does not have.

From time to time, she glances at the woman who is staring at her. Tries to read her expression, which is enigmatic. She senses a furious determination on the woman's part, but also something more, something indecipherable.

Time has stopped. There is no escape.

Sweat beads her forehead. She looks up with apprehension. She tries to breathe calmly but can't. She forces herself to remain quiet, to relax, to think of something other than this insidious torment which has been foisted upon her without warning, the same torment she has been imposing for weeks now on the woman, without ever realizing it.

Jeanne feels ashamed.

When she notices the woman has closed her eyes and is keeping them shut, only then does Jeanne feel she has permission to leave.

She gets up and strides off without a backward look.

↪ 2 ↩

When the sound of Jeanne's footsteps has faded away, Magali, the motionless woman, opens her eyes.

The view won't be pretty today. The only thing she will see is a window with a crooked blind, overlooking a section of the parking lot. But she has no regrets. She has only to close her eyes to imagine the woman who, only a minute ago, was standing in front of her.

Magali is thirty-six years old, and once studied visual arts.

A year after she entered the Palliative Care Unit, her downtown condo was sold. Florence, her friend, used to sleep there when she came to town for a visit.

But Magali has asked to keep her large studio in the east end of the city. She knows she will never go back there, but when she signed the Power of Attorney giving up control over her personal affairs, she insisted that the studio be left intact until after her death.

Sometimes, in her mind, she returns to it. She can't work now. The time for projects is over. But if she concentrates hard enough, she can recall the exact smell of the place, and how the light looked at different times of the day and night. The noises.

It's where she would like to die, surrounded by the large statues that she brought to life, and grouped around the room like so many real-life scenes. *Tableaux vivants*. Why can't she end her life among her paintings, her red clay figurines, her artist's materials, her tools and books?

She remembers her own first name even if she can no longer say it to those who ask. Or use it as a reminder to those who have grown indifferent.

It is Magali.

When she first arrived, she was called Madame Coulombe. Now they simply say "Number Six."

The fact is, she is nobody now. A long blue chair they push around. A dead body refusing to rot.

A horrible case, that must be transferred from bed to chair and from chair to bed, and attached with harnesses and straps fastened to steel rods hung from the ceiling. A frail cadaver, emaciated and undernourished, hidden inside a body flooded with lymphatic fluids that endow it with artificial curves. A stranger's body, covered with smooth pearly skin. Bluish wax. Weighted down, despite everything, by the inertia pulling it inexorably towards the earth. A body that, in contrast to most corpses, goes on resisting a decent burial.

A body where nothing moves. Only the eyes and the eyelids. The rest is petrified. Mineralized. Turned to stone. Except for the brain which will remain alive to the very end. Hers, this sublimely refined torture.

A consciousness walled inside a body that has decided to burn all its neurochemical bridges, one after the other. Limbs are filled with molten lead. Abdomen and thorax mummified. And above this body, a face permanently frozen in an expression that has no name, that is a total absence of all expression.

꒰ 3 ꒱

Number Six is suffocating. Choking. Tries to cough, in her own indescribable way. A guttural sound that rattles the rigid walls of her shrunken glottis where suddenly air, saliva and mucus converge. The diaphragm can no longer produce the little impulse needed to inhale.

It is nighttime. Magali is alone in her room.

At the nurse's station, her distress call has just been heard.

Everyone expects Number Six to choke, especially when she is lying down.

Silently, the nurses make their way to her room. They pause in the corridor, with backs pressed against the wall. Breathing softly.

Waiting.

The jerky, chaotic breathing finally stops. Completely. Stills to nothing. It always takes a while.

Silence returns. A different kind of silence.

No one moves. No one goes in. They wait. Death does not set in quickly, instantly. It takes time.

Air may not be getting into the lungs of Number Six, but her eyes will still be wide open, in a final plea. Her eyelids trying to flutter, in a final cry.

It is not yet time to go in. It's not over yet. If they were to go in now, they would be overcome by the tormented, imploring expression. It has already happened several times. And it's unbearable. Devastating. So it's better to wait outside.

For a long time now, they have been waiting for Number Six to die.

On this ward, patients usually last only a few days. At worst, they hang on for a few weeks after which they bow out, not always gracefully, but the vast majority have the delicacy to leave within the prescribed length of time.

Not Number Six. She has been here for a year and a half. She should have gone long ago to the Long-term Care Unit. When she came, no one predicted this outcome. The prognosis for such a disease rarely allows for a reprieve.

When she was admitted, she seemed at death's door. With each passing day, she continues to hesitate at death's door.

For those around her, this is burdensome. It's almost impudent of her still to be alive. At some level, this must be her choice.

In the beginning, she could still talk, in a low, hoarse voice. She could move her hands a little, her fingers, her head. She could type on a small keyboard. When she felt strong enough, she would draw, with red chalk, on a pad that lay by her right side on the bed. But nowadays she chokes more and more often, on bouillon, soup, puréed food supplements and baby food. Or when she's just trying to swallow her own saliva. She sometimes gets so hungry that she wants to cry, while at other times she gasps for air, like someone slowly drowning.

Up to now, for Magali, the worst has been witnessing the gradual paralysis of her body, as if, under her very eyes, a trocar were slowly draining away the contents of her limbs, stomach, chest, leaving her emptied and inert.

But all that has been just the prelude to the sordid horror story in which Magali, totally conscious, slides towards asphyxiation and death.

Unless something is done to avoid it. Or, at the very least, to postpone it.

It would be possible to help Magali eat and breathe. Very possible. All she needs are two minor operations: a tracheotomy to connect her to a respirator, and a gastrostomy to feed her through a catheter inserted directly into the stomach.

Afterwards, she could live a long time and, with a little luck, still be around to witness the total atrophy of her muscles, not to mention the ulceration and necrosis of all contact points between her body and the bed, the pillow case and chair. She could survive long enough to undergo total paralysis of the hands, fingers, neck, vocal cords, tongue and even lips, to the point of total aphonia. If she lasts long enough, she can observe the unbearable suffering of her family and friends, watch as they gradually pull away, and eventually abandon her.

Knowing the consequences of prolonging her life, the doctors nevertheless have suggested both operations to Magali. Not to have done so would have seemed inhumane when these possibilities existed.

Magali has refused. Clearly and firmly. Unequivocally. The torture has gone on long enough, for her and everyone else.

In a way, her decision comes as a relief to them all. Now, no one has to openly admit to wishing her a quick death, most likely by asphyxiation in a fully conscious state. Even such an end seems preferable to a slow descent into the unimaginable and unspeakable outer limits of her disease.

Magali, for her part, knows perfectly well that in her refusal of the tracheotomy and gastrostomy, she is rejecting procedures that could slow the natural evolution of this fatal disease.

Which means: no more IVs to hydrate her body and soothe the growing deficiencies caused by malnutrition; no more periodic oxygenation to counter the gradual poisoning of her blood and bluing of her skin; no more siphoning off of her saliva and phlegm during the choking spells.

All that remains is Palliative Care, designed to cheer her up as she waits to die by strangulation.

The caregivers of her unit still wash her, rub her body with soft almond oil and hamamelis, tend to the delicate needs of her mouth, apply creamy balm to her lips; move her from bed to chair so she can enjoy the spacious, newly renovated solarium; take pains to spoon-feed her bouillon, liquid supplements and sugary water several times a day; change the bandages of her increasingly ulcerous bedsores; inject the prescribed medication which means searching her body for a new vein, inserting a butterfly before the vein bursts or necrosis sets in. Every day they prepare her, psychologically and spiritually, for death. They provide support to those close to her, and coach them to deal with her imminent passing. Come to her side when she shows signs of being about to slip away. Start the distress procedure. Repeat the same scenario, a few days later. And several more times again. Secretly resent her for not dying. Feel themselves losing patience. Begin dreading the thought of having Number Six on their shift. Slowly detach themselves, avoid looking at her, stop taking the time to make contact with her. Convince themselves that she feels nothing because of the tranquilizers. Increase the dose, sometimes, without justification, in the hope of delivering her, and themselves, from this Evil.

Not out of cruelty or barbarity, but because there are levels of tolerance that cannot be reached without leaving behind one's reason and one's soul, despite the best intentions in the world.

Powerlessness in the face of such prolonged horror can drive a human crazy.

For caregivers, the dying person mirrors the possibility of their own possible decline, their own death.

Over time, if there's no escape, a human being builds up an armour of indifference so as not to feel moved, or shaken to the core, or sucked in by the violence of so much suffering, particularly the kind that refuses to end.

Not only does Magali not die, even though she is in a semi-permanent state of asphyxia, but, for over a month now, she seems to be finding ways of adjusting to her ongoing agony.

Her ulcerated bedsores have begun to heal. As if her body had made up its mind to seal the breaches and preserve the life inside. Between crises, she is still short of breath, but now her breathing is more regular. She has found rhythm in this chaos. The blue of her skin has grown milkier. Her saliva is much less abundant and no longer burns her lips, her chin and her neck. Her body is less tense in its inertia. The nurses no longer need to place rolled face cloths in the palms of her hands to prevent the fingernails from puncturing her flesh.

No one has an explanation for these changes. Except for the bedsores, which are being treated with an experimental cream normally used on severe burns.

No one is terribly thrilled about these improvements. Not in this unit, where the paradigm is progressive deterioration leading to total annihilation. Number Six has no right to settle down here, in the antechamber of Death, as if she intended to linger forever.

There is already too much despair here. So many physical and emotional tasks to accomplish for those who arrive for Palliative Care almost entirely devoured by cancer or some other horrifying scourge, and who carry, inside their small suitcases, the absolute certainty that they will not leave alive. And also for those who love them, and who will see them melt away before their eyes until there is nothing left on the bed but a frail replica of the loved one. Then, nothing. A painful memory in their hearts.

Performing the same tasks devotedly with each of the patients is exhausting. The ritual can go on for several days. At most, a few weeks. Any longer is inhuman. Patients ought to know when it's time to leave.

In the hall, the nurses wait for Number Six to die. Finally. Once and for all.

If they enter the room too quickly, one look will suffice to give back Number Six her humanity. And well as themselves.

Which would be to nobody's advantage. Things are already as agonizing as they can get. Where death fails to finish its work, a human is left in a helpless state. Everything becomes blunder, breakdown and slow massacre.

It's like trying, and failing, to kill a horse to put an end to its suffering, and after each botched attempt, the horse's eyes look up, even more terrified.

This martyrdom must cease. For all concerned.

Waiting. They are all waiting. Even those who are not here, who have loved Magali and still love her, also wait, with the caregivers whose backs are pressed to the wall in the hall of death.

When finally they are ready to go into the room, they start by switching on the ceiling light. Its raw glow reassures them.

The body lies absolutely motionless. Just as before. But that means nothing. The eyelids are closed, wet with tears. These must be the last excretions – or so they imagine for just a moment.

But they are wrong.

Of late, tears have been sliding down the waxy face more often. A disorder of the tear ducts, associated with the disease's advance. Nothing more. No one believes Number Six can still cry.

Yet that is precisely what she is doing right now.

They check her pulse.

Magali is still among the living.

She lowers her gaze so as not to see the mixture of shame and disappointment on the faces of the nurses who come into her room after their long pause in the corridor.

ᕫ 4 ᕬ

The motorcycle skids on wet pavement while negotiating a curve at high speed. The young motorcyclist is thrown into time-space and ends up on a stretcher in the Trauma Department where tonight Jeanne is on duty. He briefly regains consciousness, but can't remember his name, what day it is, or what month.

The spine appears to be intact.

The skull is fractured. A slightly indented fragment of bone from the left temple, about the size of an oyster shell, is loosed under the scalp which has split at that spot. The cut has not been sutured. The thread-like trickle of blood prevents formation of a haematoma which would compress the brain and destroy precious cells, if this hasn't already happened. The neurosurgeon will attend to it. Later.

The open fracture of the left leg will also be taken care of, later. A pressure bandage has been applied and the leg is immobilized on a plate.

Jeanne focuses her attention on the rigid abdomen. Her instructions are brief, precise.

Now she is rushing to the operating room.

In the early days, Jeanne loved conditions of extreme stress, sought them out for the rush of adrenalin that boosted her energy and mental agility tenfold. After a preliminary examination of the man's external signs, she prioritizes, and springs into action. It is not always the obvious threat that captures her attention. The real danger often lurks hidden. Like this abdomen which is hard as a rock.

Nowadays, Jeanne prefers carrying out planned procedures to emergency surgery. Only occasionally does she work in the trauma ward, replacing colleagues on vacation or at conferences, or in case of a work overload.

At forty-three, Jeanne has not yet found what she is searching for in life. She doubts she ever will.

Despite this, she continues to perform surgeries. Because she must. Because she is good at it. And also because she experiences a deeply stirring sensation when, after the long sterilization procedure, she stands at the operating table, scalpel poised a few millimetres above a living body.

She can't help but feel she is trespassing when, with a sure and precise gesture, she slices through skin and pries open the flesh. Once again she has dared to penetrate the inscrutable, sacred envelope of life, dared to dip her hands into it like a priestess at a sacrificial ceremony.

The instant the blade slices into the peritoneum, blood begins to spurt.

Everything drowns in blood. A tube siphons it off while Jeanne removes large gelatinous clots. Her fingers fumble for the submerged organs. Almost immediately she locates the source of the haemorrhage. The spleen has ruptured under the shock of the impact. She will have to grope blindly in this red mess for the splenic artery, and clamp it off as quickly as possible. But her hands are grasping through nothing but red mush.

In the operating theatre, machines are humming, metal instruments clicking and there is an uninterrupted flow of words – concise, exact, stripped of sentiment – despite the fear seeping into the stomachs of everyone standing around the table. Threatening to explode at the first opportunity. But not now. Everyone knows this is not the right time. Jeanne has located the origin of the haemorrhage and is exerting strong hand pressure to check the flow while she struggles to see clearly. But now the nineteen-year-old man's blood pressure is in free fall, and the forced transfusions are not giving him the volume of blood needed to keep him from dying on the operating table.

The machines are going crazy. Bent over the yawning stomach, Jeanne presses as hard as she can with both hands to compress the artery that she can neither see nor feel.

They have packed the abdomen with gauze compresses and are removing them, blood-soaked, to make room for more. At last, the flooding stops. The organs start to emerge. Still, Jeanne knows if her hands relax their pressure the tiniest bit, the cavity will be swamped again.

The volume of blood must be stabilized, the cardiac rhythm regulated, so the blood pressure can climb before she proceeds with the operation.

The trouble is, there is not enough time.

The monitor sounds an alarm. On the screen, the heart line is no longer dancing erratically. It's not dancing at all. It has flat-lined. And despite all their efforts, the electrocardiogram has levelled out as well.

Death is in the room, on this table, in this shattered young body. They can smell its wild animal smell.

Everyone falls silent while they go through the final, mandatory motions. Jeanne pulls away from the table. She peels off her latex gloves. Soaked and stained with blood, they snap in the silence. The machines have stopped humming.

She has one more awful task left to perform. But not here.

The mother of the young motorcyclist has arrived. She sits, alone, in the waiting room, which is always empty at this late hour.

☙ 5 ❧

The remainder of the night has been relatively quiet. Jeanne is lying down in the little room reserved for the surgeon on duty.

She watches the dawn push back the shadows. Her head is empty. She feels nothing.

Her mind has switched off some circuits, as it does every time she encounters death in a living body that she has just opened up.

As it does on every occasion when she has had to announce to relatives that there is no longer a person living inside the much-loved body.

Each time this happens, she witnesses the pain surge through them, as if she had performed an amputation without anaesthesia.

Jeanne ends up sinking into a deep sleep, marred by a dream in which she drops something – she doesn't know what – that she absolutely must hold on to. It is soft, formless; it undulates in her hands. And yet, when it falls to the ground, she hears the crystalline sound of a bulb breaking. She wants to look at it, examine it, but her eyelids are sewn shut. The dream repeats itself, ad infinitum.

She wakes up, exhausted. Takes a shower and prepares to do her rounds on the fifth floor.

Everything feels empty and absurd. Her work, her life. Existence in general.

Before entering each room, she braces herself, takes deep breaths, throws back her shoulders, puts on an air of confidence.

This morning, she doesn't talk much. She confines herself to the essentials. Cutting short the complaints of patients who are not seriously ill, and who don't need major surgery. The ones who just want to parade their aches and pains, as if she could do something about them.

Jeanne does not have surgery this afternoon. After her rounds, she will be free.

She could work out, swim, walk on the mountain or go rollerblading for hours, as she often does to rid herself of stress, to silence her thoughts and to keep her body in top condition. But today she is not up to it.

She would rather not go home on a day like this. If she retreats behind the walls of her apartment, she will only sink deeper into herself. Even books are not much help when she feels this way.

At the nurses' station, she adds notes to the files, adjusts the prescriptions. Dr. Arsenault, her best friend, puts his hand on her shoulder and whispers a few words about last night. Luc is one of those who understand. Experience has smashed his vanity, mowed down any illusions of omnipotence. He is also the only man that Jeanne has ever loved.

Jeanne touches his hand and bows her head, her throat in a knot. She refuses to cry. She rarely cries, even in private.

Last week, when she broke down in front of the woman with Lou Gehrig's disease, it was totally unexpected. She doesn't know what overcame her. She had no reason to cry.

She has not gone back to see the woman.

๑ 6 ๑

Jeanne is climbing the stairs, but stops on the landing to lean on the windowsill.

She's not sure whether this is a good time to go to the west wing of the sixth floor. She is feeling vulnerable.

And yet, the only thing she wants to do is see this woman who is immobilized.

She had thought her totally helpless, this patient who had inspired only vague curiosity and condescending concern, until she challenged Jeanne with her eyes and stripped her naked.

This is why she fears going back.

She is even more afraid that if she waits too long, there will be no one left inside the body in the big blue chair or on the bed in Room Number Six. Perhaps even now that body has been reduced to ashes, buried. Unless it is lying in the morgue in the basement of the hospital, or on some slab, awaiting autopsy.

Jeanne continues walking upstairs.

Passing through the sliding doors of the unit, she acknowledges the staff around the nursing station, then proceeds down the corridor.

She arrives at the entrance of the solarium, and stops: the blue chair is still there, off to the right. She sees only the high back. She leans on the door frame, and breathes a sigh of relief.

The woman emits a sound which, though guttural, is not aggressive. On the contrary. She knows Jeanne is there. She has heard her step. She has been waiting for her all week.

Even though she can't yet see the face which is turned the other way, Jeanne greets the woman and approaches the chair. She wheels it around, and sits down in an armchair opposite her.

Silently, the two women face each other.

"I was afraid I wouldn't see you anymore," says Jeanne.

The woman closes her eyes for a moment, then opens them. Tears sparkle in the corners.

"I didn't know if you wanted to see me after what happened."

The eyelids flicker rapidly, once.

Silence.

"Your anger was so fierce the other day. And it was justified. I'd been observing you for weeks and moving your chair around without even asking your permission."

Jeanne sees a trace of that same fury in the woman's eyes.

Silence.

Jeanne lowers her head.

"I didn't realize that you were there, really there."

The anger in the woman's face intensifies. When Jeanne looks up, she feels the full force of it.

"What? What did I say?"

The woman still looks harsh, judgmental.

"What is it?"

Heavy silence.

Jeanne straightens up, leans forward, and rests her elbows on the armrests.

"All right, I get it. I knew you were there. Otherwise I wouldn't have moved your chair so you could see the park and the river instead of the parking lot or the wall. I apologize. I was afraid. That's all. Afraid of finding myself confronted by such terrible suffering and not being able to do anything about it."

Prolonged silence.

The woman's expression softens.

"How could I know in advance you had such a temper and that you would shoot me down with just one look?"

Jeanne suspects that the woman is also smiling. Her eyes are just a tiny bit more closed, and appear almost slanted.

"Is that a smile?"

A rapid flicker of the eyelids.

The woman, mute and motionless, lowers her eyes and glances to the left, looks up at Jeanne, lowers them again, raises them.

"Do you want me to touch your hand?"

Jeanne touches her hand.

Two blinks of the eyelids.

"Do two blinks mean no?"

One blink.

"Don't you want me to touch your hand?"

The eyes continue their game. They are not really focussing on the hand.

Jeanne moves up towards the wrist where she discovers, under the cuff, a hospital bracelet. She bends over to read it.

"Magali. Your name is Magali."

One blink.

"Magali."

☙ 7 ❧

The river is calm. The lights from the opposite shore project streaks of silver and amber across the surface of the dark blue water.

Jeanne has not used her apartment terrace for a long time now. Even though she has lived in this building for almost four years, she is not a homebody. In fact, she prefers to do her reading in cafés, parks, libraries or wherever she stops during her walks. Anywhere but here.

Hours spent poring over a palette of colours for the walls of her apartment, frantic shopping to find just the right furniture, rugs, lamps, dishes, to create the right atmosphere – this kind of activity is alien to her. Apart from a few paintings and rare objects that she has brought back from abroad, everything is white, stripped down, almost monastic. Her apartment is a stopping-off place between activities, a place to sleep.

In the past, all she needed was a studio. But since she no longer goes abroad for several months to work, she can't bear to feel cramped. It's like choking. So she has rented a very large, sunny five-room apartment, with a wonderful view that she rarely enjoys, but that at least gives her the impression she is not in a cage.

The air is fresh, almost cold. Jeanne is lying on her lounge chair, a woollen blanket pulled over her.

She tries not to move. She is playing at being Magali. But she can't quite do it. She's incapable. She scratches herself. Pushes back a strand of hair. Tugs the blanket up under her chin. Wiggles a leg. She wants to fetch another glass of wine, but forces herself to lie still instead. She pretends she can't get up. She is Magali.

She looks at the river, instinctively turns her head to watch its meandering, turns her head back, stares straight ahead, tries moving just her eyes in order to broaden her field of vision, imagines herself condemned to hours, days, weeks, months, years spent observing this part of the river. Or a wall. Or the ceiling.

Jeanne gets up, goes in and pours herself another glass of wine. She drinks it while standing in the kitchen. It would be fairly easy for her to put Magali out of her misery. Maybe that is why Magali has established contact.

It wouldn't be the first time, for Jeanne.

She did it several times when she was abroad on humanitarian assignments and someone begged her to end their, or their child's, interminable agony.

Here, it is much riskier, more closely controlled in the name of a code of ethics that, under pretext of exposing abuse, sanctions horror. A suffering dog is put down without hesitation when nothing more can be done for it. But not so for a human being, even though he or she begs for mercy. Society turns its back, allows nature to slowly devour flesh, innards, heart, along with the remaining fibres of courage that hold a tortured body together. Right up to the bitter end. We pretend this interminable butchery entails no suffering. Zero pain. Anyone who intervenes is a murderer.

If Magali is able to express her desire to die, if she clearly asks for Jeanne's help, she won't hesitate for one minute. Regardless of the circumstances.

Standing at the mirror, Jeanne passes a hand over her forehead, nose, cheeks, her lips, chin, and neck, as if she were touching someone else.

She has rarely been comfortable in her own skin, this armour of dermis and epidermis in which she feels claustrophobic. This thin, obstinate frontier that marks the limit between what is her and what is not. Inside and out. The waterproof envelope enclosing a body's secrets which Jeanne, despite her disillusionment, still opens with her scalpel because she hopes to find the place where life, and the person, lie hidden.

ॐ 8 ॐ

Ever since the age of eleven, Jeanne has felt like a stranger in her own body. At eleven, the superb, adored child suddenly metamorphosed into a massively obese, graceless teenager with a forehead pitted with acne. All because of a hormonal disorder that was diagnosed and treated only three years later.

Up until then, life had been easy for Jeanne. People always liked her immediately, unreservedly, at home and at school, without her having to do anything but be herself. This didn't make her vain or manipulative. Life held no mysteries, and she thought naively that everyone was like her.

In the space of a few months, she turned into a monster. She no longer recognized herself in the mirror. This couldn't possibly be her body. She didn't want it. She loathed it.

She would burst into tears, throw a tantrum at the drop of a hat. Wouldn't eat or made herself vomit. Refused to leave the house except to go to school. The rest of the time she shut herself up in her room.

At first, despite their bewilderment and worry, her parents tried to downplay the problem. They told Jeanne that growth spurts and weight gain were not unusual during adolescence. That it was only temporary.

Jeanne countered that she knew nobody to whom this had happened. That none of her friends were like her. That she was the only one to suddenly become so fat and ugly.

The slightest thing could set her off. New clothing. Meal time. A television show, an ad, a film, a magazine showing young girls who were all slim and beautiful and surrounded by boys. Family reunions when cousins would stare at her open-mouthed. Their sympathetic comments would make her fly off the handle and act rude.

Her friends started to pull away from her though they tried not to show it. But Jeanne saw everything. Heard everything. Let nothing go by. After many futile confrontations, she ended up totally alone.

At home and elsewhere, no one could talk to her. As soon as her father or her mother broached the subject, she would begin screaming. It was if she was struggling to free herself from a straightjacket.

She forbade them, above all, from telling her she was.

Most of all, they were forbidden to tell her that she was not freakish-looking; that she looked worse in her own eyes than in reality; that she still had lovely eyes; that it would be better if she smiled; that they loved her as much as before; that she was just a little chubby.

She was not "a little chubby." She was obese.

This body had taken over her life.

It was as if she, Jeanne, were no longer there.

She was sure of one thing. Her parents didn't love her anymore.

Her father used to call her *My Sunshine, My Pet Lamb, My Beautiful Jeanne*. Now he simply called her *Jeanne*. Despite his best efforts, he had become more distant with her. He felt uneasy in her presence, less inclined to take an interest in her.

Sometimes, he found himself staring at a stranger – the kind of child that he would never have wanted.

To no avail, her mother did all she could to keep Jeanne from losing faith – to no avail. Was it because she herself had trouble believing this was only a passing phase. Jeanne's aggressiveness finally triggered hers.

Secretly, she blamed her daughter for all the upsets she was causing in their little family, and between her and her husband. Now practically all conversations turned on the subject of Jeanne. They often disagreed on the seriousness of the problem, the attitude they should adopt, the measures to be taken. Each was tempted to put the load on the other's shoulders and quietly slip away. They started to dread, and at times delay, returning to the house after work or an outing because the atmosphere was so charged. As if their overweight Jeanne now occupied all the space.

Their family doctor was no help at all. They talked Jeanne into seeing him, but the consultation turned out to be just one more humiliation. He made her undress, bit by bit, in her mother's presence, to identify the main areas where fat had accumulated, which he measured with callipers. He examined the ganglions, heart and lungs. Jeanne was so embarrassed that she sweated profusely. She came out of the examination totally mortified at having exposed her despised body not only to the doctor but also to her own mother.

The blood and urine tests showed neither diabetes nor any other anomaly other than a bit of anaemia. According to the doctor, the problem was adolescence, which is tougher for some than for others. She just needed to watch her diet, get some exercise, take iron supplements, and use a special cream for her acne. And because Jeanne seemed to have difficulty accepting her physical changes, he suggested that she see a psychologist.

She went three times. Each time, Jeanne openly refused to answer the psychologist's questions and maintained a stubborn silence. Occasionally, she interjected: "My only problem is this body. I don't want it."

When she graduated from grammar to high school, teachers who didn't know her classed her with kids who had psychological problems: pathetic cases, social rejects. She became easy prey for small daily acts of violence. She endured the name-calling – fat-ass, stupid, meathead, mongoloid – and became the kind of person that nobody wanted next to them in class or as a teammate, least of all as a friend. She was never invited anywhere; they would steal her packsack, her bicycle, and even hide her clothes in the gym cloakroom. She was openly laughed at, and sometimes pushed around in the corridors, outside in the school yard, or on the bus.

Jeanne never spoke of the harassment, the small persecutions, the physical abuse.

She never denounced her tormentors.

Instead, she joined their ranks.

In the evenings, in her bedroom, she would slowly sink the sharp point of her compass into the fat of her stomach. Or slash her thighs with her Exacto knife.

Her body had betrayed her. It was her enemy. It had to pay the price.

One day, she decided to finish with it, once and for all.

At the hospital, after her attempted suicide, the doctors finally discovered the cause of her obesity.

෨ 9 ෪

The path is deserted. Jeanne has one more hour of steep climbing before she reaches the top.

Each step demands an effort. This is how she likes it. But this morning, she is tired and the mountain is not re-energizing her as usual, despite the crystal clear air and the fragrance of the undergrowth. Her body is resisting, hindering her steps, making its presence known. And she can't stand it.

Jeanne is beautiful. People turn around in the street to look at her. She is forty-three years old. She has mastered her body, brought it under control.

When she was fifteen, once the pituitary gland problem was identified and treated, she took revenge on her body. She subjected it to rigorous training, a balanced, if austere, diet and implacable discipline. It became her object and she would never again be at its mercy.

When Jeanne entered college, those who had not known her before saw her as warm, likeable, outstanding. They courted her to join their little clique. They wanted to be counted among her friends, to please her, to be as much like her as possible. Those who had known her in high school would say bizarre, damaging, things which nobody believed. Instead, they just discredited themselves.

Nowadays, Jeanne still does a lot of sports and maintains a healthy diet so her body will go on obeying her and functioning at peak level. It's no longer so important to be admired by others.

For years, she did her utmost to bring people under the spell of her charm. So they would not look down at her. She wanted to be loved.

This was her revenge.

But it couldn't compensate for the past. Her efforts to inspire mystery, fascination, desire, or envy cut her off from people as much as when she had suffered from paradoxical obesity and water retention.

Jeanne is having trouble following the rocky path. She can't seem to silence her thoughts.

She quickens her pace, pushes herself forward, wanting to break down her resistance. To dominate not only her body but also this rebellious spirit that has kept her isolated, even in this, her appealing new form

Jeanne wants to stop thinking of the mute, immobilized woman whom she obsesses over. She wants to smash that mirror.

Magali's loneliness reminds her too much of her own, even though Jeanne has done all she can to change. Even though, unlike Magali, she can move, talk, work, travel, surround herself with people. Laugh.

Many men have caressed her body, slid into her, penetrated her. Some have even tried to touch her heart. But they never found Jeann in this lovely body, presented like a decoy.

A lovely stone pigeon. A stool pigeon.

Jeanne had genuinely loved Luc Arsenault but she had never allowed herself to say it, nor did she believe that he loved her, though he did. She kept him at bay.

After a three-year affair, she broke it off, convinced that he would leave her if ever she became obese or ugly.

⊃ 10 ⊂

The solarium is crowded.

It's often like this on Saturday afternoons. Conversa-tion, tears, laughter are less muffled than during the week.

There is as much laughter as tears. Not only from the visi-tors, but also from those who are dying. You can't always be cry-ing and anyway, people want to laugh. Even inside a wasted, dis-figured body, there is still life, the essence of a sentient being which can't help but thumb its nose at death.

Magali, too, is laughing, or her eyes are. She didn't expect to see Jeanne here today.

Jeanne is not wearing her green hospital gown. Which means she came to the hospital just to see Magali.

Normally, Magali hates Saturdays and Sundays. People are more inclined to stare at her, observe her furtively. They discuss her in undertones. They pity her, but never come near, never speak to her, never look at her directly.

Nearly every Friday evening, Florence comes to see her, but everything has become so difficult that Magali prefers to spare her friend. When she sees Florence come in, she closes her eyes and acts as if she is no longer there. Florence speaks to her softly, strokes her hands, her head, her face. She stays about an hour. Because Magali does not respond, she leaves early.

Those who spend almost all their days and sometimes even nights sitting by their soon-to-vanish loved ones are very different from those visitors who only come once a week, on a Saturday or Sunday.

These occasional visitors are ill at ease, and don't know where to look, what to do, what to say. They often end up acting as if nothing is wrong. They speak of anything, of the news, their problems, the weather, their projects. But inside, they are looking forward to the moment when they can leave and go home and cry without restraint. They berate themselves for not having really said goodbye, for not saying the important things, for being so afraid of their own vulnerability.

The soon-to-die are slow to take offence. They understand. They have come to understand many things, in pain and silence. It is enough that these people, moved by their sick ones' approaching demise, have shown the courage to come and see them one last time, to speak to them, kiss them awkwardly upon arrival and again when they leave.

Jeanne didn't make it to the summit of the mountain this morning.

From her packsack, she retrieves a few leaves coloured by autumn. She shows them to Magali one by one. She rubs them gently between her fingers, near Magali's ears so she can hear them rustle. Passes them under her nose, and brushes them against her skin before depositing them on her knees.

She takes out a tiny red berries that she rolls around in her cupped hands.

Ferns, somewhat faded, with soft spores under the fronds.
Cones that are prickly and gummy.
A clump of rabbit fur that she slides along Magali's neck.
Thick, spongy moss.
Acorns.
Partridge feathers with which she caresses Magali's cheek.
Rich black humus.
Little pine and spruce branches, full of sap.

A big mushroom, soft as velvet, that she cut away from the trunk of a tree.

Magali studies each one. She recognizes the texture, the wild smell.

She can hear the mysterious sounds of the forest. The cracking of branches. The rustle of leaves. The murmur of water as it rises from the ground, secretly, and trickles among the stones. The stirring of animals moving about discreetly, unseen. The sharp cry of a squirrel surprised to see someone in his backyard. The explosive sound of a partridge as it flies off, wings beating.

Jeanne takes Magali's hand.

They are walking in the woods together, their eyes closed.

꩜ 11 ꩜

The staff in the Palliative Care Unit suspect that Dr. Deblois is no longer coming to the solarium just to take a break, as she used to in the beginning, but because she is interested in Number Six.

Her two visits this weekend, and the private meeting with Dr. Plourde, Magali's physician, confirm their suspicion.

Some think that it's just a professional interest, but those who saw Jeanne speak with Magali, touch her, give her presents, know that something much more unusual is going on.

They also notice how Magali has changed in the last two weeks. She seems less obstinate in her silence, less strained in her immobility. She no longer lowers her gaze at their approach. She even makes eye contact. It has been many months since she has done that.

This unexpected revival intimidates them. She is visibly improving.

There is no longer any distress, supplication, or reproach in Magali's eyes when she looks at them. She communicates a *Hello* or a *Thank you for still looking after me*. The staff all feel it, and it makes their work a little less difficult, not so futile.

Even before conferring with one another, they have started to call her Madame Coulombe again. They are positioning her chair at a better angle in the solarium. Moving her at noon. Remembering to ask her if everything is all right. To which Magali always replies with her eyes. One blink for yes. Unless they are rough with her. They are also moistening her lips more often. Asking her to evaluate, by blinking, the degree of her discomfort, from one to ten, using their fingers which they unfold one by one. And adjusting her medication in response.

There is still a person inside this crucified body. They had all managed to forget that. Magali had done her share to help them forget.

When she first arrived, she could still talk a bit, in a low voice, and type a few words on a keyboard. They would listen to her attentively, bend over her to follow the movement of her lips. They positioned her fingers on the keys so she could communicate as much as she liked. They asked about what she had said or written, and came up with hypotheses in order to better understand what she wanted to communicate.

But, little by little, her voice grew fainter and her fingers escaped her control. When they tried to read her lips, they found the movements too weak, too faint to make out the words.

Magali became very impatient. She would groan like a beast because no one understood her. She would shed silent tears, refuse to swallow the spoonfuls of sugary water or bouillon that they would force into her mouth, roll her eyes furiously to make them understand what she wanted.

☙ 12 ❧

One day, Magali's physician arrived with a chart on which the letters of the alphabet were printed, in five lines and six columns.

	6	7	8	9	10	11
1	a	b	c	d	e	f
2	g	h	i	j	k	l
3	m	n	o	p	q	r
4	s	t	u	v	w	x
5	y	z	.	?	!	/

He explained to Magali how it functioned.

When using the tablet, Magali's caregiver runs a finger along the top line of numbers from 6 to 11, slowly, all the while looking at Magali's eyes. When Magali blinks, she stops. Whatever letter Magali wants is somewhere in that descending column.

Then, the finger moves down the left-side column, from 1 to 5, until again Magali blinks. The letter she wants is at the crossroads of that line and that column.

3 and 9 means P.

1 and 6, A.

2 and 8, I.

3 and 7, N

5 and 11 means the end of the word.

P-A-I-N. PAIN.

Then come the questions, to clarify the message. Magali blinks with each question, once for yes, twice for no.

"Are you in pain?"

One blink.

To escape the silence of the grave, she immediately adopted this laborious means of communication with a kind of frenzy. Her caregivers had to pay close attention to the exact moment when she blinked. Sometimes, they lost the thread and had to start all over. Magali would end up exhausted and angry. Often they forgot, on purpose, that the chart existed.

Eventually, after several tries, staff members simply gave up. Their workload was already intolerable without this additional burden.

Dr. Plourde had suggested, for her more immediate needs, that Magali just use words, preferably short ones. *Bed. Thirsty. Back.* Or just coded beginnings or juxtaposed words: *Fl come* for *Telephone Florence and ask her to come.*

It was more efficient but it reduced communication to practically nothing for Magali.

In the beginning, Florence, her friend and former lover, had been coming and spending hours and hours with Magali in response to the latter's irrepressible need to communicate. But the whole process proved to be very laborious. Moreover, Florence lived and worked in another city, a hundred kilometres away.

Before the illness, distance was nothing. When they felt like seeing each other, one or the other would make the trip.

After the diagnosis, when Magali became more and more incapacitated, and found out the doctors had given her only a few months to live, Florence took a sabbatical to be with her.

Months went by.

When the sabbatical was over, Florence went back to her job.

Florence still came as often as she could when Magali was first admitted to the Palliative Care Unit. She spent all her free time there. Magali was always on the point of dying. From one day to the next. From one month to the next.

Florence became exhausted, physically and mentally. She lost a lot of weight. She slept badly, had trouble working.

She began hoping the hospital would phone and tell her the crucifixion was finally over, that Magali was resting in peace. So that she, too, could rest.

But instead, the communication chart made an appearance. In a final effort, Florence answered Magali's call.

Their painful meetings were so constrained and exasperating that a hateful tension began to grow between the two women.

Magali panicked, thinking that without the chart, she would soon be walled in total silence. She didn't realize that her determination to communicate at any price was destroying the only relationship she had left.

When Florence came down with a bad bout of the flu, Magali finally realized that her friend was totally exhausted. Florence remained at home for nine days, recuperating.

As soon as Florence walked in, Magali saw how drawn, thin, and sad her friend looked.

This time, with the chart, Magali simply said: "I love you."

From then on, Magali abandoned the long messages. Sometimes they only exchanged a few words before Magali would close her eyes and pretend to sleep so that Florence would not feel obliged to stay.

Magali was losing strength. She was almost always asleep. She no longer asked for the chart. She opened her eyes only rarely.

Florence started spacing her visits farther and farther apart.

ꙅ 13 ꙅ

The purpose of Jeanne's meeting with the doctor has nothing to do with medicine. She wants to know more about Magali before her illness, her life and the people in it.

Dr. Plourde is not pleased that Dr. Deblois, a physician from another section, is so interested in his patient.

Does Dr. Deblois want to put an end to this woman's suffering? She has the means to do it. But if someone found out, the suspicion would fall on his shoulders.

Or does she want to help Magali renew contact with the outside world? As if everything hadn't already been tried to ease the patient's emotional suffering. Perhaps Dr. Deblois imagines that she can do better. Perhaps she is unaware of the massive amount of energy that has been poured into caring for Madame Coulombe.

When he finally decides to talk to her, he begins by cautioning Dr. Deblois against a form of dangerous compassion that he also experienced intensely during the first months when he was looking after Madame Coulombe. Such an attitude implies a refusal to accept the ferocity of such an illness, a stubborn desire to prevent the patient from sinking into an appalling but absolutely inevitable solitude. In his opinion, it was better to focus on helping Madame Coulombe accept reality than mislead her into believing she could escape it.

If he could have delivered her woman from this awful situation, he would have done it long ago. Dr. Deblois knows as well as he does the limits of medical intervention.

On the other hand, devoting too much time and energy to this patient because one cannot endure the thought that nothing can be done for her, would only harm her in the long run. Such over-concern cannot be maintained for very long. Eventually, one is faced with one's own powerlessness and despair. There are others to look after. Other tasks to accomplish. And one must live one's life, like everyone else. Little by little, a physician has to distance himself, and of course the patient suffers. This leads to guilt at having abandoned her after giving her so much attention. In fact, by trying too hard, one has only made her solitude more excruciating. In Madame Coulombe's case, all this attention may even have slowed down the inevitable process, preventing her from letting go before reaching such an advanced state of degeneration.

Jeanne prefers not to pass judgment on the doctor. Nor does she question his point of view. It is his own, and likely the result of painful experiences with Magali.

In the past, Jeanne has sometimes had to detach herself from close relationships with certain patients either because she was too busy, or had to go abroad, or simply because she could not face the inevitable outcome that loomed ahead, despite all her efforts.

With Magali the situation is totally different. This time it has nothing to do with her being a physician, or believing that she can save Magali.

She is the one who needs Magali.

She needs to know this woman. To get close to her. To help her, Jeanne, break through her own isolation.

She doesn't feel she can say this to Dr. Plourde because there is something almost indecent about it.

How can she ask a woman who has been stripped of everything, including speech and the use of her body, to give up one more piece of herself?

☙ 14 ☙

Jeanne is assisting Luc in a delicate operation on the digestive system of a three-month old baby.

The most difficult part is over. Everything has gone well. After more than an hour of concentration, conversation has started up, light and relaxed.

Out of the blue, Luc asks Jeanne why she is interested in the woman on the sixth floor, the one with lateral amyotrophic sclerosis.

Jeanne's hand pauses in mid-air, over the baby's stomach.

News certainly travels fast.

She changes the subject and continues her careful work.

Afterwards, when they are alone in the room beside the operating theatre, Luc reminds her she has not answered his question.

She knew he would bring it up at the first opportunity. He is tenacious. Even after their break-up three years ago, he never really detached from her. By sheer force of perseverance, he has become Jeanne's best friend now that he can't be anything more.

"She moves me. That's why," answers Jeanne.

"That's dangerous."

Dr. Plourde must have spoken to Luc. They're both trying to dissuade her from visiting Magali.

Jeanne doesn't want anyone else involved in this affair. It concerns only Magali and herself. It is a private matter. If Magali doesn't want Jeanne to visit her, she can always make it clear. Jeanne asked her that question on Sunday. She also asked if she could meet with her physician to ask him a few questions. Magali agreed.

"You want to help her die?" Luc asked.

"No!"

Jeanne's answer is vehement – immediate. She even surprises herself.

"So what are you trying to accomplish? Nobody can help that woman."

Jeanne knows that nobody can help anybody. So little can be done, in fact, that it's laughable. How to alleviate human suffering in the midst of horror? Five years, like so many others, she was shattered.

In Kenya, at Lokichokio.

Up until five years ago, she used to go on humanitarian missions several months a year. Wherever they needed a surgeon. She reached a point where she thought she had seen everything, and was immunized against the worst atrocities.

But one day, which had begun like any other, a truck arrived with another load of severely wounded people, not all of whom had survived the transport over potholed roads. In seconds, Jeanne's defences were pulverized.

How often had she seen this look devoid of hope or expectation, this fixed stare of mute amazement, mixed with disbelief? In that pestilential truck filled with bloody, dismembered, disfigured bodies, how could anyone be sure who was alive and who was already a corpse? Especially when the flies didn't seem to discriminate?

It was probably no worse than other scenes Jeanne had witnessed before. It was hell, in its purest form, as she had encountered it everywhere. Suddenly, though, she couldn't stand it, anymore. She had overdosed on horror.

Perhaps she suddenly realized that her small efforts could do nothing to stop human cruelty. It was the sheer enormity, the speed with which thousands of people throughout the world were having their hands chopped off, their legs severed by land mines, their faces torn away, internal organs blown to bits. How they starved to death, or endured agony from diseases that are harmless in the West but fatal there. How they died for lack of medicine, adequate hygiene, food, water.

That day and in the days that followed, Jeanne did her work as usual. But something inside her had been destroyed.

She ended up calling Geneva, asking them to send another surgeon to take her place.

She persevered stoically until he arrived, three weeks later. Then she went home.

It was the last time she went abroad to work.

🌀 15 🌀

Jeanne goes to a small print shop and has them recreate a communication chart similar to the one that Dr. Plourde had told her about. He has not been able to find it in his office.

She has it mounted on a passe-partout and plasticized.

Seated on her bed, she learns to use it quickly, trains herself to remember the letters corresponding to the intersecting numbers in the columns and lines.

3 + 6 and 1 + 6 and 2 + 6 and 1 + 6 and 2 + 11 and 2 + 8 = MAGALI.

After her meeting with Dr. Plourde, Jeanne goes back to the solarium to see Magali, who is waiting anxiously.

Magali doesn't know what image of her the doctor has given Jeanne, what he said, or what Jeanne would consider important. She doesn't know if Jeanne's attitude towards her has changed, as a result.

Jeanne takes Magali's head between her hands, looks her in the eye and presses her cheek against Magali's, holding it there for a long time. Then, she sits down in front of her and places her hands on hers.

After a moment, she says, with a smile:

"I know now that you are an artist."

"And that your friend's name is Florence. And that she lives in another city."

Silence.

This is exactly what Magali wanted Jeanne to know and remember. The rest does not matter.

Magali feared the doctor would speak only of her illness. That he would refer to her as just a patient. As if she were only that, and no longer a person in her own right.

In fact, apart from cautioning Jeanne, Dr. Plourde had insisted on talking exclusively about Magali's illness, just as she had feared he would, and on the problems that such cases pose in a Palliative Care Unit. He also emphasized the time and effort spent on Magali during the first months of her hospitalization. The letter board, for example, had proved too demanding for the staff, and gave Magali false hopes although in the end it only exhausted her.

Jeanne had asked about the chart, if she could see it. After a brief explanation, he pretended to go and get it.

Seeing the doctor's resistance to talking any more about Magali, Jeanne asked him a few more questions that he had answered laconically. Either he knew very little about Magali before her illness, or he judged that this information would only feed into Jeanne's interest, which he felt was inappropriate.

Magali was a visual artist. He had never even seen her work, and yet he knew some of it was displayed in buildings downtown and elsewhere.

She had a step-brother out West, in Vancouver, maybe. Dr. Plourde wasn't sure. He had never met her step-brother.

"Magali's father died when she was little. Her mother remarried, a long time ago. She was always alone when she came to see her daughter."

"For the first few months, Magali's mother had been very present. She came every time there was an emergency, day or night. Whenever they thought Magali had reached the end. But it took days to recover from these false alarms. To see her daughter in such a state made her sick. She finally asked them not to call until it was all over insisted that her daughter not be sent to the extended-care facility. The last time she visited, arms loaded with gifts, it was Magali's birthday, back in August. Magali slept through the whole visit."

Dr. Plourde got to his feet, picked up a file, and told Jeanne he had to see a new patient.

"One more question and then I'll leave you. Was Magali living with someone? Did she have a partner? Children?"

"No. Neither partner nor children."

"Someone close to her? A lover? A friend?"

"A friend. Florence Auger. She took care of Magali. But she lives in another city and her work is very demanding. She's a geneticist. She still comes occasionally to see Magali, but since communication has been reduced to almost nothing, it's difficult for her."

"She's just a friend?"

Dr. Plourde's face and voice showed signs of a slight impatience.

"Girlfriend. And now I have to go."

✎ 16 ✎

It is three in the morning. Jeanne rolls onto her right side and stuffs the pillow under her head. A few minutes later, she turns onto her left side. Then she lies on her back, in the middle of the bed, arms crossed, eyes wide open.

She will be in surgery from eight to noon. Nothing very complicated. Routine work. But even so.

Later, in the afternoon, she has at least two hours of consultations at the out-patient clinic. Followed by rounds on the fifth floor.

Before going home, she plans to look in on Magali.

Jeanne needs less sleep than most people. Because of her work, she has trained herself to cat nap. To sleep in noisy, uncomfortable surroundings when she has to, and wake up quickly. Strangely, now that her life is more stable, now that she doesn't travel abroad and no longer works in traumatology, except off and on, she has started suffering from insomnia. These episodes usually follow a pattern. She falls asleep promptly, between midnight and one, and is woken by a nightmare between two and three in the morning. Most of the time, she remains awake until dawn, just a short time before she has to get up. This time, it isn't exactly a nightmare, though one of the scenes in her dream troubles her.

In the dream, Jeanne is with Magali, Florence, Dr. Plourde and another woman whom she doesn't know. Everything is calm and absolutely quiet.

Magali is wearing a long white linen tunic, very plain. Jeanne and the two other women are dressed the same way. Magali is seated in a straight-back chair. She is not paralyzed, but she is sick and about to die. The others are standing beside her.

Dr. Plourde hands Magali a little paper cup in which there is a liquid that looks like milk which is supposed to help her die without pain. Magali takes the cup and drinks the liquid.

Nothing happens.

Dr. Plourde disappears. Magali is looking at Jeanne. There is no panic in her expression. Only patience. She is waiting.

Jeanne hands Magali a cup which is similar to the first one, but this time it seems to be made of mineralized light. It is white, like milk, but also radiant.

Magali takes the paper cup and drinks from it.

Jeanne and the other women help Magali get up and lie down on the floor with them.

Together the four women take the form of a star, feet touching at the centre, heads pointing out.

Something strange happens. In a flash, without their moving, it is as if they all made love. One perfect moment of fusion. Indescribable.

When it's over, they remain stretched out, for a moment, feeling wonderful.

Then Jeanne, Florence and the other woman slowly stand up.

Magali remains on the floor. She is dead.

Jeanne takes Magali gently in her arms. She is light as a feather.

She notices that Magali's body has been amputated below the pelvis. Which totally disconcerts her, leaves her horrified. She hands Magali's mutilated body to Florence who takes her in her arms in an embrace.

Kneeling, Jeanne searches desperately for the rest of Magali's body.

The floor is spotless, gleaming.

The fourth woman bends down, touches Jeanne's shoulder and tells her that everything has taken place.

Nothing is missing.

ᘒ 17 ᘓ

All is quiet in the hospital. Most of the patients, including Magali, are asleep.

Magali's room is empty except for her wheelchair, to avoid cluttering the space and allow movement around her bed.

Jeanne pushes the big blue chair towards the head of the bed and sits down, near Magali.

It is the first time that she has visited Magali in her room.

It is not like the solarium in here. Everything is cold, metallic, functional. The night table and the windowsill are piled high with medical supplies. The metal rods on the ceiling, the pulleys, the hooks, the harness suspended above the bed, remind her of equipment used in slaughterhouses to move the carcasses. Jeanne knows that all this is necessary, and she has seen much worse in neurosurgery and in the severe-burn units. Still, the atmosphere in this room breaks her heart.

She removes the long silk scarf from around her neck and wraps one end around Magali's hand. She holds the other in her own hand. She leans back.

Eventually she falls asleep.

Magali is the first to wake up. She immediately notices the dazzle of a bright Naples yellow that the first rays of the sun light up on her hand.

Magali follows the flow of yellow silk which leads to Jeanne asleep in the blue chair. She can't see her well because the chair is at the extreme left limit of her field of vision.

Magali closes her eyes. She thinks she is dreaming.

Yet she feels the lightness and coolness of silk on her skin.

ꙭ 18 ꙭ

This morning, Jeanne explained her schedule to Magali, and that she could not come back before early evening.

Magali blinked twice.

"That's not alright with you?"

Again, a double blink.

Magali stared fixedly at Jeanne and opened her eyelids a little more.

This is her expression for "you" It has taken Jeanne many days to understand that.

"Me?"

Magali shifted her gaze towards the window.

"You want me to go outside?"

One blink.

Magali's eyes remained glued to Jeanne as if asking her to stop talking and pay attention.

Then they blinked again, just once.

Once again Magali looked at Jeanne, and widened her gaze. Meaning "you." Then she shut her eyes, as if she were sleeping.

"You want me to sleep? You want me to get some rest?"

One blink. Magali was squinting slightly. She was smiling.

Tomorrow, Jeanne will visit her with the new communication board.

The bicycle path that skirts the river for some twenty kilometres is lit by small English-style lampposts that create the atmosphere of an old movie. Jeanne likes this path, particularly in the evening and very early in the morning. When circumstances permit, she goes to work on foot, bicycle or rollerblades. The hospital is about six kilometres away, an important factor when she was choosing an apartment.

Jeanne listens to the sound of her skates on the asphalt.

She is alert to the easy swing of her hips.

To the supple extension of her right leg, and then her left leg.

Each thrust sways her body from side to side, smoothly, in a soft swaying motion.

Most of the time, Jeanne skates energetically to accelerate her pulse, to work her muscles and free her body of accumulated toxins and tensions, and to empty her mind of its constant tiresome chatter.

This evening, her body chooses its own rhythm and Jeanne goes along with it.

Magali's immobility has made Jeanne more sensitive to her own body, this familiar beast that she has so ruthlessly tamed because it once betrayed her during her teens. And it could do so again.

When Jeanne looks at Magali's body, she feels no anger. On the contrary, she feels a tenderness for this body gagged, constrained, captive. Because this body is Magali and she suffers.

In those places where the track is straight and smooth, Jeanne closes her eyes and abandons herself to the movement which rocks her from side to side, carrying her effortlessly forward.

The first snow fell two days ago. It melted as soon as it touched the ground but, for a few hours, large snow-flakes danced in the air.

This may be the last time that Jeanne goes skating this year. After leaving the hospital, instead of turning right towards her apartment, she headed left in the direction of the three little islands, five kilometres from the bridge and linked to the looping paths by wooden footbridges.

The air is cold, transparent, and the indigo sky is riddled with stars.

On the largest of the three islands, Jeanne sits down on a bench and throws back her head.

Each time she stares into this immensity, she feels dizzy. It's like being on Luc's sailboat, on the ocean. Or at the top of a mountain where you can see the distant summits gradually fading away in the fog.

She has always been dazzled by nature but for the past few years, she has noticed her throat tightening up, anxiety grabbing hold of her despite the elation she feels. It's almost as if all this beauty were crushing her, as if her life does not matter in the face of such infinity.

Curiously, this anxiety does not surface again at their rendezvous the following afternoon.

Instead, everything is in its rightful place. Where it should be.

Part Two

A person is a signed piece, engraved
with a hieroglyph of human genes.

— RICHARD SELZER

After talking it over with Magali, Jeanne asks Dr. Plourde and the nursing staff to reserve a corner of the solarium for the sick woman.

Magali has chosen the south-west corner. Her chair can be moved a few degrees to the right or the left to give her a view of the river, the bike path, the small park or the woods. This way, she will not be on display, or simply parked any old way.

A chair is placed beside her, and a low table on which Jeanne lays a bouquet of sweet-smelling white roses. Magali takes a deep breath of their perfume, and tastes the velvet texture of the petals on her lips.

Along with the Q-tips, the balm and the water to wet her mouth and lips, there is also a photograph of Florence and Loup – Magali's Persian cat – an unpolished wooden box about the size of a shoebox, an address book and a ring of keys.

Magali, using the communication board, has asked Jeanne to search at the bottom of her night table, and to bring her these objects.

Now she wants Jeanne to take the box and open it.

Jeanne slides back the two tiny metal clasps and opens the lid. Delicately, she removes a statuette wrapped in a square of virgin wool. The likeness of a woman.

Feeling uneasy, Jeanne looks up at Magali.

The woman is carved out of a soft, blond wood. It is probably pine. She is bound from top to bottom with a thin wire, so tight that it bites into her flesh in several places. The woman's arms are fastened to her trunk.

Magali points to the communication board with her eyes. Jeanne takes it and slides her finger over the numbers.

4 + 8 and 4 + 6 = US.

US.

Jeanne bursts into tears. She cries with great hiccups, a thing she hasn't done since she was a teenager.

Magali also bursts out sobbing, though her stomach, chest and shoulders do not move, and her features do not change. But her eyes are running and her sobs come as harsh, jerky noises torn from her throat.

After a while, Magali asks again for the board.

3 + 11 and 1 + 7 and 3 + 6 and 3 + 8 and 4 + 9 and 1 + 10 and 5 + 11 and 10 + 2 + 8 and 3 + 11 and 1 + 10 and 5 + 11 = REMOVE WIRE

Jeanne doesn't understand right away. Magali looks at the statuette.

"You want me to remove the wire?"

One blink of the eyes. Magali smiles gently, her eyes drowning in tears.

Jeanne wipes Magali's face with tissues and caresses it with her hand.

Then she dries off Magali's eyes, and helps her to blow her nose.

She takes the statuette from her lap, and using her short fingernails, she picks at the wire, pulling it from around the neck where it is embedded.

This job must be done meticulously, with patience and dexterity. Qualities Jeanne possesses. Which is why other surgeons often ask for her help when they operate on babies or newborns.

Jeanne pricks her finger. A little blood appears on the tip, which she sucks.

It's difficult work, undoing the tiny bonds bare-handed, removing them with scissors. Jeanne breaks her nails, and pricks herself again, but she doesn't give up.

The wires around the neck finally loosen, but Jeanne has difficulty unwinding them from the rest of the body. It is almost as if, with time, the wood has built up scar tissue around the wire, absorbing it since it can't free itself of it. Jeanne tugs very gently so that the statuette won't break in her hands. The neck is so fragile, the wire so coiled.

ꕤ 2 ꕤ

Jeanne tries a key, then another. There are three keys in all.

The front door of the building opens.

Five years ago, the government bought and renovated this old factory, then converted it into a cultural centre and artists' cooperative. Dance studios occupy most of the first floor except for a large hall reserved for events. The second floor is for musicians. The other two are for visual artists.

Several groups of artists opposed the choice of this building because it was out in the boondocks, hardly a stimulating environment. The government representatives claimed the budget did not allow for a building that was better situated and that, in any case, the metro was practically next door.

Magali's studio is on the top floor, facing west.

Turning right towards the elevator, Jeanne hears the muffled cacophony of little noises that blend together in a low buzzing, like a bees' hive.

A few men are struggling to get a concert piano into the freight elevator. Jeanne takes the stairs.

She has never before been in a place so totally dedicated to creation, where diverse works are being born simultaneously. It reminds her of obstetrics, the labour and delivery rooms.

When she turns the key to enter Magali's studio, Jeanne feels the same emotion as when she slices into the intimate recesses of a body.

Slowly, she pushes open the big door and pauses on the threshold.

The late afternoon sun sheds a golden light on this sanctuary, populated by large sculpted humans.

Jeanne closes the door and advances cautiously, almost as if she wanted to avoid profaning this space to which Magali has given her access.

The dust motes floating in the sunshine, the brilliance of the large paintings on the walls, the life-size statues in groups here and there, the shavings on the floor near the workbench, the enormous lump of clay to the right of the door under an untidy tarpaulin, the unfinished painting on the easel, the art materials left there as if Magali might walk in at any moment, all contribute to the sense of an immense, primitive and sacred place.

The palette is still dotted with paint, tubes and pots of paint lie open, brushes, sponges and spatulas have not been cleaned. Surprisingly, even after all this time, little dust has collected.

With a fingertip, Jeanne touches a big glob of bright red paint that has hardened on the palette.

Magali had used this mixture of purple, carmine and alzarine red to paint the canvas background on the easel. The colour is as vibrant as fresh blood.

Four women in long, soft yellow dresses are standing in the painting. They are unfinished.

Some distance from the worktable and the space reserved for painting, is a large unmade bed, as if someone has just gotten up. A t-shirt and woollen socks are lying on the floor. A big sweater and a white bathrobe are draped over a chair.

Female-looking sculptures seem to hover over the bed, protectively.

The oldest figure stands closest, bent over, the left hand extended as if to touch the forehead of a sleeping child. But at her fingertips, there is only empty space.

Another figure, seated, has her arms wrapped around a third woman who is lying, eyes closed, head bent back.

A fourth, further away, seems to be walking with difficulty, dragging a heavy burden, a formless mass of cement from which various objects protrude: a doll's arm, the broken blade of an oar, the upper part of an espadrille, a clump of hair.

On the counter of the makeshift kitchen and on the table nearby, there is a little wine left in a bottle, a glass and dishes.

One statue, standing apart in a dark corner of the room, attracts Jeanne's attention.

It's a life-size reproduction of the same statue that she loosened from its bindings. In this case, barbed wire is wound around the body, piercing it. Even the face.

Jeanne has only one wish, but Magali has not given her permission.

∂ 3 ɔ

Magali is listening to Jeanne. Drinking in her words.

Bit by bit, the studio is coming back to life.

Though she has often returned in her imagination, she could never be sure it still existed.

She has had to fight her mother and the administration of the Cultural Centre to prevent her studio from being emptied and handed over to another artist while she is still alive. There was no guarantee that her wishes had had been respected, given the length of time that had elapsed. She doesn't even dare ask Florence to drop by occasionally, as she used to. She is afraid to broach the subject.

Magali no longer asks Florence anything for fear of plunging her into the past. For fear of forcing a contact that might also mean obliging her to get on with her life, to build a new life, without Magali.

Jeanne speaks in a low voice. It's as if she has retreated into her own head.

Having entered Magali's personal territory, Jeanne suddenly finds herself without signposts, totally disoriented.

Yet, when she was in the studio, she knew exactly where she has always wanted to be: inside the heart of a human being. Jeanne has met another Magali. The immutable Magali.

Jeanne goes on speaking with intense concentration. As if she is still in Magali's studio, seeing and feeling it again. She goes over every corner, retraces her movements. Repeats all her gestures.

She remained in the studio until nightfall, and it still haunts her.

Magali is troubled by some of what she hears. A few small details do not coincide with her own memories of the reality she left behind.

Something is wrong, and this awareness slowly takes over Magali's mind. She is no longer listening to Jeanne. She is somewhere else.

After a while, she focuses on Jeanne. With an insistent eye movement, she tries to ask her for the chart, but Jeanne doesn't hear. She is too absorbed, lost somewhere in Magali's world, and her own.

Magali makes a noise that sounds like a groan, and repeats the eye movement.

Embarrassed, Jeanne runs to fetch the chart. She places her index on the number at the top left hand corner, and apologizes for her monologue. She didn't realize it might be difficult for Magali to hear these things.

Magali reassures her.

She simply needs to be alone.

There is something she would like Jeanne to do for her.

ꙩ 4 ꙫ

Jeanne leafs through the address book Magali has asked her to take home with her. She still feels bad for having talked so much about her bewildering experience in the studio. And for ignoring Magali, almost as if she wasn't there.

It was almost as if, during an appendectomy, with the patient only under narcotics and local anaesthetic, Jeanne had opened the body too wide and lost herself in contemplating the workings of life. As if she had taken the heart in her hand, just for the pleasure of feeling it beat, plunged her hands up to the wrists in the smooth curves of the intestines, reached under to touch the uterus – that sacred urn – and the ovaries – tiny vessels of humanity – without even addressing the woman immobilized on the table, her vision curtailed by the canvas that separated her head from her abdomen.

Jeanne wonders if she has broken a taboo in the studio, desecrated a temple without being aware of it.

There is a fine line that separates a sanctioned intimacy, desired by both parties, from an invasion. Or a violation.

Had Magali really wanted Jeanne to immerse herself as she had done, body and soul, in her universe? To be filled with it?

How could she really know, when Megali had only said, *Go studio address book. You see me other.*

No speak much. Happy Jeanne studio. Need alone. Address book Florence come. Thanks Jeanne being Jeanne.

Even if Magali had been able to talk freely, how could she, Jeanne, know what she thought in her innermost being? She and Luc had tried so often to talk openly, rarely finding the words to give the other access to the dark and wordless zone inside the self.

Jeanne dials Florence's number.

She gets the answering machine.

She has primed herself to speak to Florence, so she remains silent. She hangs up. Practices what she will say to the tape.

"Hello. I'm a friend of Magali's. She would like you to come and see her."

"Good-evening, Florence. I am Jeanne Deblois. Magali asked me to tell you that she would like to see you. *Au revoir.*"

Jeanne dials the number again.

This time, Florence answers.

Jeanne hangs up.

ᴂ 5 ᴐ

Florence is with Magali.

Jeanne is aware of this. She is having trouble concentrating as she listens to a patient she operated on two days ago.

Yesterday evening, Florence phoned Jeanne right after she hung up for the second time. Their conversation didn't turn out quite the way Jeanne expected.

Florence knew that Jeanne was seeing Magali almost daily, and that they were using the communication board. That Magali seemed to be doing better since Jeanne started speaking to her. That she was choking less often. And had re-established eye contact with the nursing staff.

But Magali cried more.

Dr. Plourde had spoken to Florence, and he'd expressed his reservations about Dr. Deblois' personal initiative. Magali had finally achieved some kind of peace of mind that should be protected. Dr. Plourde had advised Florence not to enter into this game, for Magali's sake.

Up until that moment, Florence had been speaking in a cool, detached way, but her voice suddenly broke, with rage, *For months now, Magali has pretended to be sleeping whenever I come to see her.*

She wept, noisily.

Jeanne was stunned into speechlessness. She knew nothing about this woman.

Between sobs, Florence blurted out:

You don't even know her!

Jeanne felt as if Florence had spit in her face, and without thinking, she asked, *If you know her so well, why don't you ask her why she hasn't spoken to you for months?"*

Then Jeanne hung up.

She barely slept that night.

Leaving the operating theatre, Jeanne went and told Magali that she had passed her mess age on to Florence. That was all she told her. She felt uncomfortable. As did Magali, visibly. Her eyes kept moving.

Pretending to be late for a meeting, Jeanne gave Megali a quick hug and hurried out of the solarium.

Jeanne passed a visitor in the corridor. In a flash, the idea came to her that it might be Florence.

Jeanne stopped and looked back.

The woman entered the solarium.

ᔒ 6 ᔗ

Jeanne pours herself another glass of wine. She shouldn't be drinking this evening. Tomorrow morning, at eight, she has surgery.

For the past three days, when not at work, Jeanne has locked herself away in her apartment. Her car has sat in the garage.

She hasn't gone back to see Magali. She doesn't know where she stands.

She wonders if Magali is angry at her. Did she transgress some boundary in the studio the other day? Jeanne had wanted to soak up the atmosphere for Magali. She wanted to bring the studio to Magali. She thought Magali wanted this as well, but perhaps she had been wrong.

Magali had never asked Jeanne to leave before.

Apart from interrupting her abruptly, and demanding to be left alone, Magali had also asked for Florence.

Also, Florence had been very direct on the phone. Jeanne had usurped her place. The place of a person who has a history with Magali, a past.

Who is she, this Jeanne Deblois, to enter Magali Coulombe's life instead of her?

A perfect stranger, who dared to push her chair without even asking permission. Nothing more.

Jeanne pictures herself growing heavier. Once again, she has become the obese girl she thought she'd left behind.

ꙮ 7 ꙮ

Two in the morning.

Luc doesn't understand what Jeanne is telling him on the phone. She is sobbing.

He says he's coming over.

When he walks in, Jeanne is curled up on the living-room carpet. She is still crying.

Luc has never seen Jeanne weep.

She says, "I've had too much to drink. You have to replace me tomorrow in the operating room."

Usually, wine makes Jeanne happy. Even at the worst of times.

It took Luc some time before he understood how she could get drunk and laugh, even after the hospital he was in charge of had been bombarded, leaving twenty-six dead and many more seriously wounded.

Or after losing a patient.

Or after a break-up.

Laughter. It is one of Jeanne's many coping mechanisms, one of the ways she protects herself. Along with work and sports. Luc knows it now. It is her way of not drowning, of exorcising the dark side of reality, the horror hidden beneath the surface of daily life, the mine always set to explode under one's feet.

That evening, drinking had made Jeanne miserable. She had finally collapsed.

Luc had always sensed her extreme vulnerability, her sadness. But he had never seen Jeanne like this before, with her defences down.

Luc helps her to her feet. He wipes her face with a wet cloth. As if she were a child.

She doesn't take her eyes off Luc. He strokes her forehead, her hair, pushes back a few strands, wipes the tears that are still trickling down her cheeks.

"How can you love me?" she asks.

ॐ 8 ॐ

Jeanne arrives in the solarium around eleven, with no makeup, her hair wet from the snow. She doesn't drop by the cloakroom before coming up to the sixth.

She has just walked to the hospital through the early December storm. It did her a world of good.

Magali's chair is turned towards the entrance. At first Jeanne thinks this is negligence on the part of the staff, but yesterday Magali asked to be placed there so she could wait for Jeanne. She tells her this.

She explains to Jeanne what happened when they discussed the studio. Why she suddenly wanted to be alone. Why she asked her to phone Florence.

The unmade bed, the coffee in the cup, and other small details had indicated to Magali that Florence still loved her. Ever since Magali had decided to play dead during her visits, the only place Florence could be with her old lover was at the studio.

Magali and Jeanne talk for more than an hour.

೨ 9 ೮

Florence is lovely, with a strange, wild beauty and a delicate sensitivity.

This was not apparent in the photo that Jeanne has seen of her in the solarium.

But Magali had succeeded in capturing her presence in the studio. She is everywhere, in the paintings, in the sculptures.

Not the actual physical person, but rather her essence.

In Magali's studio, Jeanne had the impression, without understanding why, of being inside something alive. Or, more exactly, inside a living, breathing person.

Jeanne has nursed, repaired, patched and revived broken bodies, each time hoping to save them or, at least, relieve the person trapped inside the body, a highly sophisticated organism that is so unstable, capricious, perishable.

Each time she opens up a body, Jeanne finds herself confronting the mystery of the human being buried inside, somewhere under the thin defences of the epidermis, dermis and layer of fat, inside the damp, trembling cavities where delicate viscera are lodged. If one of them weakens, and fails, the rest may follow. And when this happens, a human body suddenly turns into a cadaver, to be quickly burned or buried before fermentation and putrefaction swell and corrupt the image of who this person was, right before our unbelieving eyes.

And then nothing. Nobody. Nowhere.

In Magali's studio, there was definitely *someone*. A presence, enduring. As if Magali had succeeded in breathing into inert matter what Jeanne has always looked for in palpitating flesh. Life itself – fluid and intangible. The human being, not caged in a body, but circulating freely through the centuries, from generation to generation, from body to body.

Florence, suddenly intimidated by the way Jeanne is staring at her, stops talking.

"What is it?" asks Florence.

Jeanne looks down.

Silence.

She looks up at Florence.

"It's you."

⊙ 10 ⊚

Magali would like to live out the little time that is left at the studio. With Florence and Jeanne.

They hadn't expected such a request.

And yet as soon as Magali expresses her wish, they start to visualize it, despite all the difficulties and logistics that such an undertaking will entail, and the consequences for each of them.

They think about it for two weeks. They talk about it. The two of them. The three of them.

Little by little, in their minds and conversations, it becomes evident that this extravagant fantasy could become an actual project, providing concrete solutions to precise problems.

Finally, they feel ready to undertake the risks and move in together in the studio. For different reasons, they all need to.

Jeanne informs Dr. Plourde of their decision.

To him, the idea is totally crazy. It's beyond him.

What is the merit of moving Madame Coulombe to a place that is totally inadequate for her needs in her present condition?

Sometimes patients on the brink of death want to move back home, rejoin their world and their loved ones. This is understandable. Most of the time, however, they know that such a move is impossible, a fantasy that cannot be realized. They no longer have the strength left to deal with the slightest change, and usually they stop short of imposing such an ordeal on their loved ones.

In Madame Coulombe's case, it is even worse. Not only because she is paralyzed and can't talk, which in itself demands ongoing and special care, but with her prognosis, she could live another six months to a year. And furthermore, she has already defied all the prognoses.

If she were to leave Palliative Care, it would be out of the question for her to come back in two weeks, one month, or three months, should Dr. Deblois change her mind and find the case too difficult. Madame Coulombe would then have to go to a long-term care unit, whatever her state of health.

"I am ready to sign a discharge. Anything you want. I take full responsibility for this case."

Dr. Plourde is taken aback by the sheer folly of this plan. Dr. Deblois, a surgeon with a reputation for being cool and logical, is ready to interrupt all her activities for an indeterminate period, to look after a paralyzed woman who is about to die.

"In any case, this is Magali's wish and we intend to respect it."

"It is not up to you to decide her fate. Nor up to her girl-friend. Not even the patient, given her incapacity. Her mother should make this decision. She has all the legal rights."

❧ 11 ❧

Reine has never accepted Florence.

In fact, she is deeply disturbed that her own daughter loves another woman. Before Florence, Magali loved men. She was normal. In a way, that had reassured Reine.

Magali might be an artist, which Reine didn't appreciate, but at least she was seeing men. Even though most of the time she was seeing painters who didn't have a nickel to their name, let alone talent, according to Reine. Not to mention writers who couldn't make a living.

Florence's request doesn't surprise Reine, but she finds it outrageous. Luckily, Dr. Plourde has warned her what they are planning behind her back.

Reine's position is clear. Magali is no longer in any condition to decide what is best for herself. She lost contact with reality a long time ago and can no longer communicate.

This incapacity is not really such a bad thing where Reine is concerned. But of course she would never admit it to Florence.

Magali no longer has the power to torment her with that old story that Reine thought had been buried long ago. When Magali fell ill, she had insisted on digging it up, and used it to attack her mother even more doggedly than before.

Rather than have her come back to life, Reine would prefer Magali to remain straitjacketed in her silence until she dies. She hopes that day will come soon.

And yet, when Magali was little, they had loved each other. They had been like two accomplices, before Magali started to say terrible things about Paul, Reine's second husband.

In her attempts to destroy her mother's second marriage, Magali had been motivated by jealousy.

She hated the thought of Reine-Aimée remaking her life, and allowing Paul to rupture the little cocoon the two of them had built around themselves after the death of Magali's father a few years earlier.

It was even worse that Reine-Aimée, her "Dearest Mummy," was about to bear this man's child.

It was during this pregnancy that Magali started to change and invent those monstrous tales.

As if Paul, who never refused them anything, and had introduced them to a dream life they would never have known otherwise, could possibly have abused Magali.

Reine could not allow Magali, with her only-child machinations, to be so possessive and egotistical, and destroy the precious happiness that Reine was finally experiencing.

So Magali is better off locked in her crypt where she can no longer upset Reine, and make her ill just as she had a year and a half ago. What would be the point? Magali is going to die. Why excavate a past that has been carefully buried for all these years under thick layers of silence? If everything gets dug up again, as Magali hopes, and an old nagging doubt is transformed into certainty for Reine, what will happen to her once Magali is gone? How could she go on living with Paul? Or alone, for that matter, knowing the awful truth?

Because even if Reine could defend herself against her daughter's repeated attacks and was able, at whatever the cost, to save her marriage and her family, Magali had still managed, right from the start, while Reine-Aimée was carrying Bertrand, to inject her with a terrible poison – doubt.

Reine does her utmost to silence this doubt, to muzzle it, to cover it up with convoluted arguments with which she deceives herself, though not her daughter.

Florence listens to Reine discourse, pontificate, babble, and finally declare that she will not allow anyone to disturb her daughter after has fought so hard to prevent Magali being transferred to long-term care. She trusts Dr. Plourde completely, and he is very familiar with Magali's case. Had she known, she would never have allowed Magali to keep her studio. She would not have negotiated with the administration of the Cultural Centre. She would never have made all those generous donations. There is no going back in the past, and Reine is not about to be fooled once again. It is out of the question for Magali to leave Palliative Care.

Florence despises Magali's mother.

She is horrified by the elegant and charming facade behind which this woman hides her misery, her falseness.

She is even allergic to the sound of her voice, obsequious, false, and the deluge of words she uses to mask the cruelty of her silence.

From adolescence on, Magali stopped calling her mother her *Darling Mummy*, her *Reine-bien-aimée*.

Her mother became plain "Reine," disloyal and unjust. Unworthy.

From the time she reached voting age up to the time of her illness, Magali cut off almost all contact with her mother. There were two exceptions, Christmas and her birthday, when Reine insisted on giving her outrageously extravagant presents.

Magali accepted them all, without offering anything in return. This attitude did not offend Reine who thought she could cleanse her conscience little by little by regularly making offerings to her daughter, under the guise of exemplary indulgence and exalted generosity.

Though she had nothing to do with the terrible illness attacking Magali, she couldn't stop herself from thinking that somewhere she might bear some responsibility for the horrible fate that had befallen her daughter. Though she never admitted it to anyone, she couldn't get it out of her head.

To combat the terrible anxiety that kept growing as Magali's symptoms multiplied and worsened, Reine had decided to do everything in her power to support Magali in her ordeal, until death finally delivered her. Afterwards, it would be too late to make amends, to tell Magali how much she loved her, despite all that had driven them apart.

At the time, Magali was feeling devastated by the news of her prognosis. Her world was starting to shrink. She had the impression that the muscles and bones of her legs, especially in the left one, had emptied out and were slowly being replaced by an icy, viscous tar. More and more, she found she was limping, tripping over her feet, losing her balance as if sinking into mud, falling down for no reason. She had cramps and painful twitches. She could feel the sickness rising, invading her hips and along her left arm. She was being walled in, inside her own body.

When Reine had approached her with open arms, Magali had felt a visceral need to find her real mother. The one she had known as a little girl, and had lost.

For several months, Magali believed in an unhoped-for rapprochement, an ultimate reconciliation with her mother.

Reine was determined to repair the past. She did everything she could. Except to speak about the past. Except to admit what had taken place.

Magali brought her to the edge of a confession, so close that Reine had almost given in, opened up, confessed. At the last minute, Reine reared back and from then on kept her distance, while continuing to do everything "that had to be done" with false solicitude fed by fear and a bad conscience.

From then on, Reine refused to look at Magali. She had wished her to die quickly so that nothing would ever be spelled out between them. If it had, Reine could not have gone on pretending. Her life would be forever changed.

Florence is glaring at Reine. She would like to kill her. The woman's capacity to dissemble while saving face, makes her furious.

"At least you owe her that much, after having refused to admit that your husband abused her, under your own roof! And you knew all along!"

Reine was not expecting such a direct confrontation. She was used to hedging, to hiding, to pretending nothing had happened. She was taken aback.

Even Magali had always tread carefully over this terrain, for fear of seeing her mother break down in front of her, as had happened at the time of her father's death, when she was six.

"Do you love her or not?"

Silence.

"I only ask one thing. Only one. Go and see your daughter."

♋ 12 ♋

Reine-Aimée hasn't slept for two days.

Paul, her husband, is worried, but Reine-Aimée doesn't tell him about her meeting with Florence, and doesn't talk about Magali. She pretends her insomnia is a reaction to a new medication that her doctor prescribed. That it will pass.

The last few times that Reine visited her daughter, many months ago, Magali was in a comatose state. Completely unresponsive.

She was as good as dead, in Reine's eyes. Her body was still there, but Magali had departed and would not be coming back.

But, according to Florence, she has rallied. With all her awareness and her implacable lucidity. Her memory and her suffering included. And her extraordinary will to go to the end.

Florence was direct and brutal with Reine, who is now devastated. Florence did not spare her. She has laid things out just as they are, not giving her a chance to sink into twisted justifications, or drown the facts in a deluge of words.

But what has upset Reine most, was hearing the truth spoken so crudely by a person other than Magali. As if it were a *fait accompli*. Now that Florence has let the cat out of the bag, there is no getting it back in.

Reine-Aimée can no longer tell herself fairy tales. She can no longer pretend. She does not have the stomach for it.

Her life and Magali's have been mined by a reality that Reine has stubbornly insisted on keeping buried, even when Magali struggled to unearth and defuse the deadly charge.

More than a year ago, Magali brought her to the edge of an avowal, but Reine was not ready.

She was tied up in her petty calculations. Her reasoning went like this. If she were to admit, to herself and to Magali, that she knew what had happened, even if she asked her daughter for forgiveness with her whole heart, Magali would still die regardless, and she, Reine, would lose all. Not only would she lose her daughter, but also the security she had acquired by marrying Paul.

Magali would be gone, and Reine would be left alone at an age when it is better to have someone. Not only that, but she would have to live with the shame of not having repaired the damage she had done to Magali.

Reine-Aimée is beyond that now. She knows that she lost everything a long time ago, despite appearances.

She wants only one thing: to find her daughter before it is too late.

❧ 13 ❧

Reine-Aimée comes back from the hospital, exhausted, her coat open despite the cold. No scarf or gloves.

On her way to see her daughter, she thought she would collapse. The stress, sadness and pain completely gripped her.

Back at home, she locks herself in the bathroom, and vomits. Paul knocks on the door. He thinks Magali must be dead. He tries to comfort his wife.

Reine has often vomited before, on the many occasions she has returned from the hospital after being called to Magali's deathbed.

When this happens, Paul always pampers Reine for a few days, takes her out to dinner, lavishes her with attention to distract her.

But today, nothing can make her forget what she has lived through.

Her meeting with Magali turned out to be simple, surprising.

Reine-Aimée sat in front of Magali, and, for a long time, they allowed their eyes to speak of their boundless pain.

Then the words came spontaneously to Reine-Aimée. Honest words.

Reine-Aimée can't understand why she remained silent all these years. What she tried to preserve appears worthless compared to what she has denied Magali and herself.

When she comes out of the bathroom, she wards off Paul's comforting embrace.

Calm and inflexible, she stands facing him.

"It's over between us, Paul."

She goes upstairs, packs a bag, and leaves without another word.

Paul follows her into the street, begs her to speak, not to leave him, but it is too late.

Nothing will buy off Reine-Aimée anymore.

෧ 14 ෧

Reine-Aimée has signed all the papers. She shows them to Magali. She is laughing and crying. Then she shows them to Florence and Jeanne, as if to prove she really has done it.

Something extraordinary is in the air. An exaltation, a love that makes these women glow.

ᘒ 15 ᘓ

Florence has been able to negotiate a few weeks off from the university, after setting up a precise experimental protocol so her assistants can continue their research in her absence.

Even though this period away is tacked onto the Christmas holidays, both administration and her colleagues fear her research may be compromised again. Florence's work has received large grants since she acquired an international reputation. During the past two years, she has taken a lot of personal time off to look after her sick friend, as well as stress leave to recuperate.

Florence feels something remains unfinished for Magali. And for herself, as well.

Magali has given her time to renew her strength, to recover from the hellish period they lived through, to grow accustomed to the idea of her death. And one day, her own death, and Jeanne's, and Reine-Aimée's. The difference is that Magali's is more predictable.

Florence starts packing.

Other than the essentials, she is bringing a few things that have marked their history together. Landmarks that guided them step by step over difficult terrain that they once had to negotiate separately. They found a space where they could each be themselves, together with the other. Sheltered from whatever lies in wait outside. A place of consolation. A place where one can be fully alive, despite the difficulties. A true place.

When they first met eight years ago, Florence bought twelve clay statuettes from Magali. She places them inside a wooden box.

Every autumn, when a hundred artists open their studios to the public for a few days, Florence used to come to come to town on a pilgrimage.

She would always rent a room at the same inn, facing a large park, some ten minutes from downtown. There, she felt at home. It was where she stayed when she came to see Magali in Palliative Care after the latter's condo was sold. She couldn't bring herself to sleep in Magali's studio once Magali was no longer there.

At the public library, a directory was handed out to visitors, listing all the artists and a map to help them find the various studios. Florence had picked up the guidebook and the map on a Friday, as soon as she arrived in the city. That evening she planned her itinerary for the next two days. There were certain studios she returned to every year either because she liked the work of the artists, or because she had formed ties that had nothing to do with their work. Certain studios also fascinated her. In her itinerary, she always included a few artists whose work she had never seen.

These pilgrimages to the studios, like her numerous visits to art galleries and museums around the world, were fuelled by the same quest that had pushed her towards genetics.

At fifteen, Florence had found out accidentally that she was an adopted child. Even before she had proof, she had always suspected it, although the family never treated her differently from her two elder brothers. She had never lacked for love, and their home environment was always wholesome, full of warmth and laughter.

Nevertheless, she was shattered by the sudden revelation.

Later, despite numerous attempts, she never managed to trace her biological parents. Around the middle of her twenties, she gave up the search. But an emptiness had installed itself.

Up until the time she met Magali, she often studied her hands, face, and body, and wondered what was truly her own, and what was inherited from parents who had disappeared, without leaving a name or an address. She couldn't understand how her parents could have abandoned her, given her away, when she came from them.

Genetics nourished her, helped her to move on from her personal story to more far-reaching questions.

Isn't the individual the Great Work, the miraculous result of an almost infinite line of people who, two by two, intermingled their bodies and their genes for millennia? Did it really matter who these people were? The result was an individual unlike any other on earth, despite hereditary defects which were preserved and passed down from century to century; each was a brilliant work of art, and the mutations that happened here and there, over time, were simply personal initiatives, like an artist's signature left on the genetic heritage of the human race.

Or was the individual merely the vector of genes, like a vulgar mosquito?

Was each person simply stuck in the restricted identity of his or her distinctive genetic imprint? Isolated among a crowd of individuals, each one solitary, separate, and unable to come together except by uniting their bodies so that their genes meet, and marry?

Or is the individual *all the others* who bore them down through the ages, but more than that, is the individual the bearer of all humanity? Could each individual be a repository, sacred but transient, of everything that humans feel inside, whatever their age, their sex, their race, the place and era in which they live?

Art offered Florence answers that she could not find in genetics, despite her years of hard work.

When Florence walked into Magali's studio that day, something happened inside her.

First, she saw Magali. That was the initial shock.

Magali was walking up and down, like a caged beast, not looking at anyone in her small studio where already there were four visitors and where there were only tiny works on display. Paintings that had to be viewed up close to be understood, statuettes grouped randomly, composing a sort of narrative.

Eventually, the four visitors left.

Magali stopped pacing and looked at Florence.

"I apologize. I can't stand people coming into my studio as if it were a factory, and making comments, asking me why I do this or that. Why is my work so small? Why don't I make real paintings, real sculptures? They're invading my space! This is the first time I open my studio, but I'll never do it again. This kind of thing is not for me."

"All you have to do is put a sign on the door saying that the studio is closed. I'll be going now."

"No. Stay!"

Silence.

"I'll just go down and leave a note on the door."

Silence.

"Please stay. At least look at what I've done."

Silence.

"You're not like the others."

Silence.

"I'm not sure why."

Magali picked up a drawing pad and jotted down a few words. Then she went down downstairs.

Florence started to look at Magali's work. Her attention was drawn to a group of twelve statuettes.

Each one was meticulously formed. Each one had a different face, a singular attitude, a specific identity. And yet they only took on meaning when they were all together.

Florence stayed a long time.

ཉ 16 ཕ

Luc is head of surgery. He can organize a replacement for Jeanne by consulting the other surgeons. Christmas is approaching; there will be fewer operations. After this slow period, if Jeanne can come back to work, he will find a solution.

He listens to Jeanne. He doesn't understand what has happened between her and the woman with lateral amyotrophic sclerosis, but he senses that Jeanne's interest in Magali is not just a whim, not just a confused attempt to atone for her sudden flight from Kenya and subsequent disengagement from international aid work.

He was at Lokichokio when Jeanne asked to be repatriated before the end of her contract. It was not the first time they had worked abroad as a team.

On that day, in the space of a few hours, he saw Jeanne utterly transformed, yet he was unable to explain the exact reason for this turnabout, this sudden closing-off. She remained just as efficient, just as fast and tireless as usual, but she was made of stone. She was like a machine. An automaton.

Each time there was another emergency, another catastrophe, the whole team always came together in perfect harmony, as if each one's vital rhythm depended on the others to gather the speed that allowed them to do what would be impossible under normal circumstances. Talk was reduced to a strict minimum, gestures had to be precise and coordinated while decisions were made on the spot, without discussion, sometimes with only an exchange of looks, or a nod of the head. They were no longer individuals – nurses, physicians, surgeons, assistants of all sorts – each in his or her own space. Suddenly they were a team. This cohesion allowed them to tolerate extreme pressure, to support whoever might be weakening under the stress of exposure to extreme human suffering, and give that team member a little more strength and courage, and also a sense of meaning and purpose so they could continue, humbly, to do their part.

That day, however, Jeanne suddenly lost all faith. She was no longer one of them.

Even Luc had not been able to give her the push needed to make her stay. And yet she was the one who had fired his enthusiasm for such adventures. On their first mission, she was the one who had steered him through the most difficult moments, when feelings of helplessness had dragged him down.

Despite being warned numerous times by the humanitarian organizations, new aid workers often arrived full of ideals, only to leave a few weeks, or even days later, after colliding with a reality totally unlike their dreams of saving the world.

Sometimes, they came during periods when there was no emergency, just regular, day-to-day, routine maintenance of a nutrition centre or field hospital for refugees, when what they really craved was to experience danger, risk their lives and do great deeds on behalf of humanity. Their duties might turn out to be simple, thankless, essential rather than showy, maybe even absurd and contradictory because politics are often that way.

Other times, they found themselves face to face with human misery, crude, naked, raw, rather than masked by the media images that had impelled them to sign up. Here too, their vague heroic notions ended up shattered on the ground.

In some cases, they left because they couldn't stand the insects, sweltering heat, scorpions, monsoons.

However, even veterans like Jeanne could also sometimes break down. It usually happened overnight, without any warning signs or obvious reasons.

As if, suddenly, they realized that their job consisted in rolling an enormous boulder to the summit of a very high peak, along with other bare-handed labourers. They knew full well that once up there, or even on the way, the boulder would roll back to the bottom where new rocks were accumulating, indefinitely, with little hope that one day it would stop.

These old timers knew that the golden rule was to keep their eyes riveted on the job ahead, on the people they had to look after, such as the dying child who still needed water, milk, food, antibiotics and medical care.

But without warning, they were stunned, devastated by such a hellish vision. The mountain that they were trying so hard to climb step by step was in reality a gigantic mass grave, growing bigger daily, a scene of disaster where the few survivors were scrambling to extract themselves any way they could.

And all because of man's universal, inextinguishable, insatiable insanity.

For a brief moment, through the eyes of a few massacre victims crowded in the back of a truck, Jeanne caught a dizzying glimpse of this huge graveyard where millions were still moving, suffering, staring in disbelief at the ghastly, man-eating monster that was crushing them and all those they knew and loved. At the same time, it also had devoured those they thought they hated with a millennial hatred, as well as the many others whom they knew nothing about. Enemy bodies were piled together with their own, still alive although they might as well have been dead.

Despite her determination and effort, Jeanne could not recapture neither the innocence or the pragmatism that she needed to continue her work abroad.

Luc suspects that Jeanne has never forgiven herself for leaving this mission behind, and that she may have invented a new mission for herself.

In fact, he has the impression that Jeanne is not really "looking after" Magali. Something else is going on that he can't put his finger on.

All he knows is that Magali has changed Jeanne. As if she has given up living inside a bunker, sheltered from some imaginary danger. Before, she would rarely come out of her blockhouse, always cautiously and never for very long.

Jeanne is finally emerging. She is living without defenses.

Luc listens to this woman who moves him so deeply.

☙ 17 ☜

Magali hasn't slept. She is exhausted. She almost choked twice during the night. This morning, she is short of breath, and her skin is blue-tinged. She is icy cold.

Jeanne covers her with several blankets and places little electric pads everywhere on her, on her stomach, her groin, her underarms. She orders an oxygen cylinder even though it is written, in large red letters at the top of each page of Magali's file, *No Oxygen*.

Luc went to find a machine that would suck the mucous from Magali's throat.

When Jeanne had arrived with Luc to prepare for Magali's transportation by ambulance, they had found her in a complete panic. She was terrified.

Because her condition was weak, she was afraid her transfer to the studio would be considered impossible, beyond her strength, not to mention Jeanne's, Florence's and her mother's. Even worse, she was afraid they would think she had changed her mind, and that last night's crisis was her body's way of showing her change of heart.

Last night's choking and insomnia must have been the result of overexcitement. She had felt so happy, like a child the night before an eagerly awaited event.

Finding Magali in this state, Jeanne wondered if they had let themselves get carried away by a crazy dream. Magali might die before she even crossed the threshold of the Palliative Care Unit.

Once her breathing stabilized and her body warmed, Magali asked Jeanne for the communication board.

Magali tells Jeanne that she is willing to go. Jeanne reassures her friend, promising Magali that she will be transferred as soon as her breathing regains its rhythm.

Florence and Reine-Aimée are waiting at the studio. They are preparing for Magali's arrival. They are expecting a delay, but they fear that if this delay goes on, Magali will die without them.

Jeanne slips the CD into the player. It's the one Magali loves, Boccherini's *Stabat Mater* for soprano and strings. She puts the earphones on Magali's ears.

Luc is seated a little distance away, near the window.

Magali closes her eyes while Jeanne starts to gently massage her feet and marbled legs in order to improve the circulation and accelerate oxygenation of the cells.

Magali relaxes, she lets go.

⊃ 18 ⊂

Towards the end of the afternoon, as the stretcher is being carried out of the ambulance, Magali asks Jeanne to stop a moment, before going in, so she can remove the oxygen mask.

The snow is falling softly, in big flakes, onto her face.

The air is fresh. Noises are hushed and the lights along the street form a long necklace of cottony haloes.

Her medication has been adjusted after last night's episode to ensure a smooth trip. Magali feels like she is floating, as if she were sliding from one world into another.

The large doors of the studio stand open. Florence and Reine-Aimée come out to welcome her. All is murmuring and joy.

The transition from stretcher to bed is almost painless for Magali, thanks to the hoist that she once installed on the ceiling to move her sculptures. Jeanne had added a few new features so that Magali could be moved. In her missions abroad, she often had to resort to ingenuity to make do with what was available. Here, as well, she has tried to respect Magali's environment, and to avoid giving it a hospital look with the modifications that are needed to accommodate Magali's needs. Apart from her massive bed, nothing much in the studio has really changed

The ambulance attendants leave and Florence and Reine-Aimée cover Magali with blankets, feed her a few mouthfuls of sweetened water, moisten her lips, bring up the back of her bed, speak to her, caress her head, her hands.

Luc has never met Magali before this morning. He passes the day with her and Jeanne. Now he can understand why Jeanne is so attached to this woman. Something radiates from Magali even though she is imprisoned inside her body. This quality strangely resembles what he notices in Jeanne, a magnetism that has kept him by her side regardless of her reserve, her withdrawal, her retreat. He bends over Magali and kisses her forehead. Then he tells her that it is a privilege for him to have spent this day with her and Jeanne.

Magali slowly lowers her eyes and then raises them.

She is able, once again, to express the intensity of her feelings in a single look. Luc is troubled by the force of their communication.

Jeanne accompanies Luc to the taxi that awaits him downstairs.

She is exhausted. So is he. As if they had just spent the last thirty-six hours in the operating room, working side by side in an emergency situation.

They stand for a long time in a motionless embrace.

When Jeanne goes back upstairs and opens the door of the studio, Florence and Reine-Aimée are still with Magali. Jeanne is happy. She wants to leave them so they can all be together again. Also, she needs to be alone. She goes down the stairs feeling light-hearted, and takes a long walk under the peaceful snow.

❧ 19 ❧

The first day is difficult.

Reine wants to run the show. Because she signed the release papers, she feels responsible for Magali's happiness as well as for everything else.

She wants to reorganize the studio to make it more functional. She wants to determine who will be with Magali, at what time and for how long.

And she hates cats. She doesn't understand why Florence has brought Magali's cat here. She wants to get rid of "Wolf" as soon as possible, on the pretext that his fur is affecting Magali's respiratory tract, especially since he sleeps on the bed next to her face.

Barely twenty-four hours have passed and Magali is already exasperated and furious. She keeps choking. She hurts all over.

She regrets having allowed Reine to come and live at the studio with the others. Her dream is turning into a nightmare.

Several times, she tries to tell her mother that it is enough, that this is not what she wants, but Reine is hyperactive, talkative, overexcited. She doesn't let Magali use the communication chart.

Jeanne and Florence hold back as best they can, for fear of provoking another scene and causing Magali to suffer even more.

They talk in low voices with Reine, who refuses to listen. She is Magali's mother and it is her duty to look after her daughter.

Florence cannot get a moment alone with Magali. So Jeanne leaves again to go walking, to read in a café, to calm down. Reine, on the other hand, refuses to budge, even when Jeanne invites her to accompany her. Moreover, Reine can't stand to see Florence on the bed next to Magali. It just isn't done!

Jeanne watches Magali closing off, sliding visibly downhill, turning blue despite the oxygen she is getting.

The second evening, Jeanne tries to create a calmer atmosphere. She puts on Gregorian chants, lowers the lights and, with Florence, starts massaging Magali gently.

Reine continues talking in the background, as she does the dishes.

After a few minutes, Reine stops what she is doing. She has suddenly remembered it is time for Magali to sip some water. She turns up the lights and approaches the bed with a small bowl and a spoon.

With her eyes on her mother, Magali utters one of those terrible guttural noises.

The bowl and spoon fall from Reine's hands.

Magali, with a furious look, asks Jeanne for the communication board.

"Write message. Reine go. Give."

Jeanne hands Magali's message to her mother.

❧ 20 ❧

Reine-Aimée feels rejected, misunderstood. She cries so hard she hiccups.

She tries to prove to Magali that she has taken responsibility for her past mistakes. After all, she has left her husband, her comfortable world where her future was assured.

Now that they are here in the studio, she only wants things to go smoothly for Magali. Someone had to take charge of everyday life. Jeanne is a good caretaker, but Florence doesn't seem to have any practical sense.

Magali decides it's time to have a serious meeting with her mother.

Florence is too angry to take on the role of interpreter or even to help with the confrontation. She leaves.

Magali tries to calm her breath. To create a little silence between them.

Reine-Aimée and Jeanne wait until she is ready.

Magali begins, but not with words. When she opens her eyes, she looks long and hard at her mother. The anger is gone. A deep sadness overwhelms her.

When she asks Jeanne to slide her finger across the chart, she is trying to reach Reine-Aimée through the thick fog that separates them.

"Mummy."

Reine-Aimée puts her hand over her mouth to choke back the sobs, then she covers Magali's hand with hers.

Silence.

"I'm sorry, Magali, I'm sorry."

There is a long silence.

Reine-Aimée starts to speak, without self-pity, in a low voice but high enough so Magali can understand what she is feeling.

During the first day, she says, she lost her head, she knows that now. She entered a state of frenzy.

She is feeling shy with Magali, whom she knows so little, after all.

And she is ashamed of the distance that she has allowed to grow between them. She has the impression that the gap is so deep now that they will never be able to close it, despite all the best intentions in the world.

Magali's world, her studio, her friends, everything is so foreign to her. She doesn't know where her place is here. Nor what she should do.

She is even afraid of the studio, with its sculpted figures standing everywhere. As if the four of them were not alone, but were with all these quasi-alive figures, who speak to her constantly of Magali, of what she has experienced, felt, believed during their many years apart.

The statue of the older woman bending over the bed where she tried to sleep last night kept her awake.

Moreover, all the demonstrations of tenderness, love and complicity between Florence and Magali make her feel uncomfortable.

And it makes her feel sad to see that Jeanne, who until only a few months ago was a total stranger, understands Magali better than she does herself, knows her needs, her desires, and how to use the communication board.

These last few weeks have made her see how her whole life has been a failure on every level, a huge lie. She has spent twenty-five years with a man who abused her daughter while she, Reine, closed her eyes. She chose to remain silent, and to pretend nothing was wrong, for fear of finding herself alone once again, as she did after her first husband died.

During that time, her daughter has slowly metamorphosed into that life-size sculpture, that woman bound hand and foot, standing there, in her studio, and Reine can't stand looking at her because it makes her feel sick, tears her apart, and she knows that in some way she is responsible, even though nothing can be proved.

There is so much sorrow and so much love in Reine-Aimée's voice and expression that Magali believes that her mother is be ing reborn before her very eyes, that they are getting back in touch, at some deep level. It now seems clear that, all these years, Reine-Aimée has rejected herself as much as she has rejected her own daughter, Magali.

When Florence returns, the lights are low again and there is total silence.

Jeanne is sleeping on the floor where she chose to install herself, among the little girl statues who are playing hopscotch.

Reine-Aimée is bending over and, with her left hand, gently caressing the forehead of her sick child.

"Florence has come back, Magali my darling. I will leave you alone now and go to sleep. Good-night, my angel."

ꙮ 21 ꙮ

With the hoist, they succeed in depositing the captive woman statue at the foot of Magali's bed.

With shears and pliers, Reine-Aimée, Florence and Jeanne cut the wire that encircles it and pierces her flesh. It is difficult work. Their fingers are bloody, despite the gloves. But nothing can stop them now.

Jeanne doesn't understand how Magali managed to wind the barbed wire so tightly around the body. It must have taken superhuman strength.

Each little piece of metal torn away represents a victory.

Jeanne is the first to climb the ladder, and free the face. Reine-Aimée unties the heart. Florence releases the stomach.

Magali is resting now, with her eyes closed. She is listening to the dry snap of scissor blades severing the bonds that have been strangling her.

ꙅ 22 ꙅ

Reine-Aimée is singing with Florence and Jeanne. She is petting Wolf, who is curled up on her lap.

He follows her everywhere, rubs up against her, jumps up when she sits down and purrs contentedly. She is touched by this tenacious attention, and she no longer objects to his presence.

At Magali's request, Florence and Jeanne went to buy up a huge pine tree that they are now decorating in an unusual way. They are having fun, squeezing tubes of paint and adding thick touches of colour here and there on the branches. Magali is breathing in the heady scent of the outdoors.

They have hung the statuettes and tiny paintings they found in the storage space where Magali kept her work before she met Florence. Magali's eyes are shut. She lets herself be lulled by the Christmas songs that she loved so much as a little girl, and came to hate, later.

She is drifting away, slowly, peacefully.

Nothing has been left out.

Finally, she can leave.

Acknowledgements

The following books were of great assistance to the author on medical issues and international humanitarian aid.

Confessions of a Knife by Richard Selzer
Marie by Georges Renault
Médecins et grands patrons by Antoine Hess
The Island of the Colorblind by Oliver Sacks
Les fractures de l'âme by Fabrice Dutot and Louis L. Lambrichs
Guide d'intervention clinique en soins palliatifs by Geneviève Léveillé et la Maison Michel-Sarrazin
Un rêve pour la vie, biography of Lucille Teasdale et Piero Corti by Michel Arseneault

Aude is the winner of the
1997 Governor General's award
and the 1999 Grand Prix
des lectrices.

Exile Editions

info@exileeditions.com
www.ExileEditions.com

publishers of singular
fiction, poetry, drama, photography and art
since 1976